SHELLA

"Vachss is a contemporary master."
— *Atlanta Journal-Constitution*

"*Shella*, Vachss' latest excursion to the American underbelly, is his darkest yet.... Vachss' characterizations are so strong, so immediate, that it's impossible to brush them easily out of mind.... And I defy anyone to remain untouched by the climax, which manages to be horrific, touching, tragic and strangely hopeful."
— *Arkansas Democrat & Gazette*

"Terse, intense and brilliantly written, *Shella* is a body-blow of a book delivered by an emerging literary heavyweight."
— *Flint Journal*

"Nex
lik

"A

"

Andrew Vachss

SHELLA

Andrew Vachss has been a federal investigator in sex-
ually transmitted diseases, a social caseworker, and a
labor organizer, and has directed a maximum security
prison for youthful offenders. Now a lawyer in private
practice, he represents children and youth exclu-
sively. Mr. Vachss is the author of several novels in
the "Burke" series, and his nonfiction work has
appeared in *Parade*, *Antaeus*, *The New York Times*,
and numerous other forums. His latest books are
Born Bad and *Down in the Zero*. He lives in New
York City.

BOOKS BY **Andrew Vachss**

SHELLA

SHELLA

A NOVEL BY

Andrew Vachss

 VINTAGE CRIME / BLACK LIZARD

Vintage Books ▲ A Division of Random House, Inc. ▲ New York

FIRST VINTAGE CRIME/BLACK LIZARD EDITION, AUGUST 1994

The Knopf edition of this book was cataloged as follows:

6108 G. H

Library of Congress Cataloging-in-Publication Data
Vachss, Andrew H.
Shella : a novel / by Andrew Vachss.
   p.   cm.
ISBN 0-679-42416-4
I. Title.
PS3572.A33s48   1993
813'.54—dc20   92-75207
          CIP
Vintage ISBN: 0-679-75681-7

Manufactured in the United States of America
10   9   8 · 7   6

for:

Doc Pomus

and

Iceberg Slim

*truth, still shining
down*

SHELLA

GHOST

The first time I killed someone, I was scared. Not scared to be doing it—I did it because I was scared.

Shella told me it was like that for her the first time she had sex.

I was fifteen that first time. Shella was nine.

◆

We bumped paths in Seattle. I was in a strip bar, looking for a guy. She was dancing there, taking off her clothes to the music, humping something that looked like a fireman's pole in the middle of the runway.

After her number, she came over to my table in the back, just a gauzy wrapper on over her G-string. I thought she was working as a B-girl between sets, but it wasn't that. Like blind dogs, we heard the same silent whistle. Recognized each other in the dark.

◆

After that, we worked Badger together, riding the circuit. I'm not real big—Shella's as big as I am, taller in her heels. She works out regular, a real strong girl. I don't do muscle—I just talk to the marks, tell them the truth. Most of them get it then—they pay the money and go away. In L.A., a guy didn't listen. Big guy, bodybuilder. Flexed his biceps, came right at me. I stopped his heart, left him there.

♦

We kept moving. Denver, Houston, New Orleans. Shella took a mark home after work one night in Tampa. Back to the motel room just off the strip. I sat near the connecting door, waited for her signal. Nothing. Couldn't even hear her voice. When I let myself in, moving soft, the room was dark. Shella was face down on the ratty bed, lashed spread-eagle with wire coat hangers, a gag in her mouth. Her back was all bloody.

He never saw me coming. In his coat I found his works—a pair of black gloves, a wad of white cheesecloth, and a little bottle with a glass stopper. He had a plastic jar of Vaseline too. I smeared it all over Shella's back so her blouse wouldn't stick to her. Told her to get going, take the car, I'd meet her later, when I got done wiping down the rooms.

When the cops kicked in the door a few minutes later, I was still there.

They threw down on me, pistols and shotguns. Three in the room, probably had backup outside. I went easy. They'd been tracking the freak—he'd done three women in the last month. Same pattern. I told them my story. A drifter, passing through. I heard the noise, went inside—he was working on a girl. We fought, she ran away. He died.

The cops did their tests. Blood tests, DNA. I wasn't the guy who did those other girls—the dead guy was. One of the detectives said they should give me a medal. He wasn't stupid—kept asking me if I might know the girl who'd taken off. The one whose blood was all over the bed. Asked me about who might have been staying in the connecting room next door.

Shella had the car, all the money, everything. I was indigent, they said, so they got me a lawyer. He wasn't much—said the only way I could help myself was if they could find the girl who'd been in the room. I told him what I told the cops.

♦

When we finally got to court, I looked straight ahead in case Shella was dumb enough to show up. Nobody said much to me—the lawyers all talked together up at the front, where the judge was. This lawyer they got me, he came back, told me they had the death penalty in Florida, said I could plead to manslaughter, how did that sound?

I asked him how much time I'd have to do—I didn't care what they called it.

After a while, I said what the lawyer told me to say and they took me down.

♦

I did the time. Quiet time, after the first week. Some wolf thought I was a sheep. I could have killed him quick when we were alone, but then there would just be another one. I know about the other ones. I said I'd do what he wanted. He said to meet him in the showers.

He was there, waiting. I turned my back to him, dropped my towel, bent over. I felt his hands on my waist, and it happened like it always does. I whipped an elbow into his throat—crushed his Adam's apple. He went down, holding his throat, trying to scream. I got hold of his face in my hands. I could feel all the bones in his skull—I could feel them start to crack. The shower room floor was hard tile. The water was coming down on us. Blood ran out of the back of his head.

I could feel the other cons come in behind me, watching. Nobody did anything. It was a crazy, wild place, that prison—they wanted to watch me kill him. I got my thumb in his eye. Pushed it through until I felt it go all wet and sticky.

The guards pulled me off. I put my thumb in my mouth, sucked on it while I stood against the wall. I knew what they would think. That I liked the taste.

The wolf didn't die—they transferred him someplace.

◆

I got thirty days in solitary. When they opened the cage, I watched for a while. To see if the wolf had friends. Nobody came.

I was a good inmate. After what I'd done to the wolf, I couldn't fool anyone in there, but they stayed away. That's all I ever want.

The work wasn't hard. I didn't talk to anyone. Didn't have any money on the books, so I quit smoking. They came around to my cell, told me how I could get cigarettes, get anything I wanted. I looked at them until they went away.

I never got a visit, never got a letter.

In my cell, I did my exercises. Not like the weightlifters,

just stretching and breathing. Slowing down inside so I could count my heartbeats.

They let me out on a Monday.

◆

You can go a long distance in three years. I'm no good on the phone, talking to people. I reported to the Parole Officer, got a job working produce.

Soon as I drew a paycheck, I went back to the bar where Shella was dancing when it happened. Sat through all the shifts, came back a few times. She wasn't there.

I walked the strip, checked every runway in Tampa. Shella wasn't dancing there anymore. One night, in one of the bars, a man offered me a job. I don't know how he knew.

When he paid me, I bought a car. Kept looking. Couldn't find her.

I did a couple more jobs for the man, saved my money. When I had a stake, I headed north to Atlanta.

◆

I don't have a picture of Shella. Just in my mind. Big girl, white-blonde hair, gray eyes. Some things she couldn't change. The beauty mark on her left cheek, just past her lips. I put it there. She wanted one, asked me to do it. I rubbed some Xylocaine into the spot, froze it with ice cubes. Burned a hypo needle in a match flame, held two fingers inside her cheek to steady it, tipped the needle in black India ink, jabbed it in a perfect little dot—my hands are real steady. Shella said she never felt it, but

I could see little things move in her eyes while I was doing it.

Her name too. She gave it to herself. She was a runaway, she told me. When she was a kid. Some social worker in one of the shelters told her she had to come out of her shell. So they could help. A shell, that's what she needed. So she turned it around, made it her name. She told me it was all she had that was really hers.

But she didn't use it with people—it was a secret she told me. When I met her, her name was Candy. A runway dancer's name.

◆

I always thought about Shella in prison, but I thought about her strong now. Stuff she told me, signs on the track.

◆

Atlanta has a strip, they all do. Shella would be dancing someplace. She wouldn't turn tricks, wouldn't have a pimp. I asked her about that once, if she ever had one. She told me her father.

I was in Atlanta a week. Bought some stuff I needed while I was looking around. I'd never find her, the way I was working. I thought about a guy in New York. I'd done some work for him, years ago. He would maybe have something for me, for how I do it—up close. I don't use guns or bombs or anything. I could see him again, maybe make a trade.

Before I left, I got a set of ID from a guy who sent me to another guy. Driver's license, Social Security card, like that. The guy asked me if I wanted a passport, cost an extra grand. I told him no.

I bought a better car, a nice Chevy, couple of years old. I paid cash, drove it right off the lot. I mostly live in it now, keep my clothes and stuff in the trunk.

◆

In Baltimore, one of the dancers came and sat at my table after her shift, hustling drinks. Told me she wasn't allowed to date the customers, she'd get fired if the boss found out. But she'd take a chance, she said, flicking her red fingernail against one nipple, licking at her lips. Because she liked me so much.

We went to her apartment. It was Badger, like I thought. She was on her knees when the hammer came in. Big guy, said she was his wife. Going to hurt me for messing around in his patch. I told him how scared I was, took my pants off the bed, handed them over so he could have my wallet. He watched my eyes, never saw my hands. The girl didn't move to help him, didn't make a sound.

Shella wasn't like that. I had trouble with a mark once. It was in Phoenix. He took my first shot to the side of the neck—I heard a crack but he didn't go down. Pulled a straight razor out of his shirt pocket. I backed off to get room to go again when Shella hit him from behind, an icepick in her hand. She stabbed him so many times I had to pull her off.

The hammer had almost three grand in his pockets, half a dozen different credit cards, a little gun with a pearl handle. The girl talked fast, said he made her do it, she was afraid of him. Showed me a little round scar on the inside of her thigh. Cigarette, she said, a present from the hammer. So she'd remember.

He wasn't dead. I could feel the pulse in his neck. I told the girl I'd have to tie her up, give me time to get away. She said she wanted to come with me. I figured she was just scared, scared stupid—if I wanted to do her, taking her out of there would just make it easier. She lived with the hammer—let the cops think she'd done him, taken off. I told her she could take one suitcase.

◆

On the highway, she wanted to stop a couple of times, use the bathroom. I pulled off to the side of the road, walked her into the bushes. She didn't try to run.

I spotted a motel just off the Pennsylvania Turnpike, circled around, stopped at a 7-Eleven, bought enough food for a couple of days, went back and checked us in.

She told me her name was Misty. A short, chunky girl, heavy thighs, breasts too big for her body. Implants, she told me—the hammer made her do it.

I told her I'd have to tie her up. So I could get some sleep, not worry about her doing anything. She wiggled on the bed, smiled at me, said a little girl like her couldn't hurt me. That was what the hammer thought about me, I told her, and she held out her hands for the rope.

◆

She woke me early in the morning. Soft, just rubbing against me. Asked me, didn't I want to finish what we started just before her man came into the room? I thought about what Shella told me once, how it's evil to hurt someone's feelings, just to be doing it. How it's worse than a beating, makes you feel like nothing. So I didn't say anything to Misty. Never even untied her. She acted like it made her feel good, made little noises in her throat, went to sleep right after.

I didn't know what to do.

I had to find Shella.

♦

In daylight, she looked older. I untied her so she could use the bathroom—there was no window in there, nothing she could do.

She came out wrapped in a couple of towels, hair all wet. Sat down on the bed next to me.

"What are you going to do with me?" she asked.

"I don't know."

"You let me go, you're afraid I'll go back to the block?"

"Your man's not dead. He's not gonna go to the cops. You go back there, he's gonna thank you for saving his life, you tell him the right story."

"You don't know him. He likes to hurt me. He doesn't need an excuse."

"So?"

"So I can't go back."

"All right. You stay with me a few days. You got friends in Baltimore? Make some calls, find out if anything's going on?"

"Just a couple of girls at work. They'd know, maybe. But they'd rat me out in a minute, there was money in it. They're mostly junkies anyway, always getting busted. I couldn't trust them."

"You got money?"

"Yes. In my suitcase. You want me to get it for you?"

"No. It's enough, get you someplace, start over?"

"Yes.

"Okay. We'll do that, couple of days."

◆

Misty couldn't drive, said she'd never learned. Shella was a good driver, but kind of wild—I always had to watch her, especially on the highway. I took the wheel all the way past Philadelphia, found another motel near Trenton.

I didn't tie her up that night. Prison teaches you to sleep light, even with the door locked. One guy, he dropped a dime on this shakedown gang, took a PC lockup, thought he was safe. They filled a plastic bottle with gasoline, squirted it in between the bars, dropped in a match. The guards couldn't get close enough to open his cell. By the time they got a hose down the corridor, he was gone. They never got the smell out.

Misty was still asleep when I woke up in the morning.

I asked her again if she had enough money. Made her show it to me. She had a few thousand. Holdout money. Shella never did that with me. I told Misty I'd drop her at the bus station, or she could come along as far as Newark, catch a plane.

She told me she had no place to go, asked me where I was going. I told her Chicago.

She said she always wanted to try it there, said she heard it was good pickings.

I told her I was going alone. She asked me, did I have a girlfriend.

I made her stay in the bathroom while I took a shower.

I could see her through the cheesy plastic curtain. She took off her clothes and we had sex when I got out.

◆

On the road to Newark, Misty was quiet. I thought about it. I don't look like much—even if she described me, it wouldn't help the cops. But the car, the license plate . . .

I'm not a good thief, don't even know how to hotwire a car. We had to get a car once, in a hurry, me and Shella. She broke in, got it started. She thought it was funny, I didn't know how to do it.

Misty looked at me like she knew what I was thinking. "You don't like to hurt girls, do you?"

"I don't like to hurt anyone."

"I don't mean that. I mean . . . *like* to hurt them. For fun."

"It's not fun."

"Maurice liked to hurt me."

"Don't go back."

"I'm not. I'm good, you know. Real good. Everybody says so. I'm good. I look better when I'm dressed up. I could go with you."

"Why?"

"To *be* with you, okay? I can make money. Dancing, whatever you want."

"I don't want anything."

She started to cry then. Soft, to herself, not putting on a show. It reminded me of something, couldn't remember what.

♦

I drove through this long tunnel from New Jersey. It let us out in Times Square, long blocks lined with hookers. They looked used.

There's a hotel there, right near the highway. I put the car in the lot, checked us in for a week.

It didn't take long to unpack. Misty bounced around— she really liked the room. Took a real long shower. When she came out, I was lying on the bed, feeling the room.

"How come you keep it so dark in here, honey?"

"I was resting," I told her. I always rest inside myself when I'm not working, but I couldn't explain that to her.

She crawled on the bed, nuzzling between my legs. "Can I buy some clothes tomorrow, Daddy? I left most of my stuff back in Baltimore."

"I'm not your daddy."

"Yes, you are. My sweet daddy. You're gonna take care of Misty, aren't you?"

I shifted the muscles in my back, sat up. "I'm nobody's daddy," I told her. Quiet and nice. "You want to buy clothes, you got money. I'm not taking care of you."

"I know I have money, baby. I showed it to you, remember? I was just . . . like, asking permission."

"It's yours, you use it the way you want, understand?"

"I'm sorry."

"You got nothing to be sorry about," I told her, and let her do what she thought would make me happy.

◆

She stayed up with me all that night, doing things. I listened when she talked, working my body around to a new clock. Where I had to look, I could only do it at night.

We finally fell asleep. When I opened my eyes, it was after one o'clock. Misty was sleeping on her belly next to me, my belt wrapped around her wrists, looped over the bedpost. I touched a spot in her neck and she came around.

"What's all this?" I asked her, pulling on the belt.

"I didn't want to wake you up, baby. So I tied myself up. I know it's stupid . . . I mean, I could get out of it and all . . . but I thought you'd feel better if you got up and saw me like this."

"It's okay," I told her. "You don't need to do that anymore."

She smiled. A big smile, like I just gave her something.

◆

She took another long shower. Put on black stockings with seams down the back, spike heels. Did a couple of turns in front of the mirror.

"You think my legs look longer in these?"

I told her they did. She shoved herself into a push-up bra, put on a little black jersey dress. I watched her from the bed.

She took the hotel key, went out. Came back in a half-hour or so, had a little paper bag with cigarettes and some cosmetic stuff, couple of newspapers. I read one of the newspapers while she made some calls.

I closed my eyes, listening to the purr of her voice on the phone. When she hung up, she put some stuff into a little purse, dabbed some heavy perfume between her breasts.

"I got an audition at four—I'm not sure when I'll be back, maybe I'll be working tonight . . . okay?"

"Okay. Leave the key with me. Tell the desk clerk you need another one for yourself, slip him ten bucks. It'll be all right."

She kind of posed in front of me. "Do I look sexy?"

I told her she did.

◆

I started looking that night. Not for Shella, for the man who could help me find her. He wouldn't do something for nothing, this man. I never expect that—something for nothing, that's a whore's promise.

There isn't a lot of street sex in Times Square. Come-ons, to get you inside. Movies, books, magazines, video-tapes. The places where there's real flesh, they always let you know. Live Girls, a lot of the signs say. Like there's dead girls in the other places.

In the live places, the girls are on stage, or behind glass. You put a token in a slot, the window opens up, the girl moves around, shows herself, says things. Your time runs out, the window closes, you have to put another token in to open it up again. When one of the watchers is done, they send a man into his booth, hose the place down, spray some green-smelling stuff around.

Some of the places, the girls come into your booth. Massage parlors, modeling studios, lingerie shows . . . they have all these names for the same things. They show it to you, you want to touch it, it costs you more money. The more you want the girls to do, the more it costs.

Come and Go, Shella used to call those places.

I passed them all by, not looking for her there. Shella wouldn't be in any of those places.

Little knots of hunters on the street too, looking for someone weaker than them to take down. Smash and grab. Police cars cruised around the blocks, blue and white. Right past guys selling drugs, saying "Smoke?" when you went past.

In the windows, big radios, the kind kids carry on their shoulders. Little TV sets you could carry in your pocket. Watches, electronic stuff. All kinds of knives, camera stuff. Sex stuff too: vibrators, fake cunts made out of fur, handcuffs, leather masks with zippers for mouths, dildos.

◆

I walked criss-cross through the blocks until I found the place where I used to meet the man. The club had a different name, but I figured, they do that all the time, he might still be there.

The beefy guy at the door took ten dollars from me. I sat down at the end of the bar. On the stage, a woman dressed like a little girl, short little dress with straps over a blouse . . . like a sailor suit. She had on little white socks, shoes with straps over the front. Dark hair in pigtails. Licking a lollipop, lifting up her skirt with one hand, pulling it down, teasing.

When the bartender came over, I asked him for the man, gave him the name I had. Monroe. I didn't offer him any money to tell me, that's what a hunter would do. I asked him like I was an old friend, been out of town for a while. Shella always said I didn't know how to be slick, but I could do pretty good if I had to.

The bartender went away, like he hadn't heard me. I stayed where I was. He came back, looked me over careful, like he'd have to describe me. I knew that wouldn't do any good—I don't look like anything.

I sat there, watching the woman on the stage bend over, flip up her skirt, pull down her underpants, crawl around so everyone could see. She had a roll of fat on her hips, lumps on her thighs.

The bartender came back again, leaned over.

"If I knew a guy named Monroe—*if* I knew him, understand?—who would I tell him wants to see him?"

I'm no good at that kind of stuff—I never know what to say. I told him to bring me a glass. He gave me a look, but he went and got one. I held it up to the bluish light in the bar. It was medium weight, had spots on it from the dishwasher. I took the glass in my hand, squeezed it until it popped, crushed the glass in my hand, put it back down on the bar—only the bottom of the glass was in one piece. I opened my hand so he could see there was nothing in it. No blood either.

"Tell him it's me," I said.

The bartender looked, said I could find Monroe in this poolroom on the East Side of town. Gave me the address, said Monroe would be there tomorrow night.

◆

I don't dream much. I did when I was a kid. In the institution. I'd wake up, wires in my face like I was screaming, but no sound came out, the blanket all wet from my body. I was always scared then.

Every place they put me, I was scared. All the time, scared. I ran away, a lot. Every place they put me. The foster home, the farm. I could always run away. The last time I ran, I wanted to get far away, so I stole some money from a store. Just grabbed it out of the open cash register and ran. They caught me so easy.

Where they put me, there was no place to run.

Every other place they put me, the grownups ran it. But in the institution, the kids ran the place. Not all of them, just a few.

Duke, he was the one in charge. A real big kid. I think he was seventeen. He was in other places before too. The way you could tell, he had two little blue blobs tattooed on his face. They were supposed to be tears. One for each time he was locked up before.

The first time I saw the tears, I thought, I guess I could get one myself now.

Duke had flunkies with him always. They carried his stuff. He never carried anything himself, not even his cigarettes. They always handed him whatever he wanted, even a knife, sometimes.

The first day I was there, I went in the bathroom. Duke was there, with his flunkies. He had one of the littler kids and he was slapping him. Hard. Over and over. The flunkies laughed. The little kid's face was all red and wet. Duke took the little kid back into the showers. I kept my face down, but I heard them. He made the little kid suck him.

I didn't say anything to anybody. I knew that much from the other places.

When the little kid came out of the bathroom, he laid down on his bunk with his face in the pillow. He was crying when The Man came by. When The Man asked him why he was crying, the little kid said he was homesick.

The Man laughed at him.

Every day was like that. Duke and his flunkies would take everything for themselves. If you were playing basketball when they came up, you had to get off the court. They watched whatever they wanted on the TV. If you got packages from home, they took some of it.

I never got any packages.

The nights were the worst part. The Man never checked on us at night. He stayed outside the dorm, watching his own TV. As long as it was quiet, he never came back where we were.

Fridays, we got our commissary draw. That's when we could spend our money. They held our money for us until then. Every week. On Fridays, you could buy cigarettes, candy, soda pop. It was supposed to last you all week. Duke took some from everyone.

Even the State kids, the ones with no families like me, they got something. For chores, like cleaning up the grounds outside.

One Thursday night, Duke and his flunkies came over to another kid. They woke him up. I kept my eyes closed, breathed deep like I was asleep. But I listened.

"Tomorrow, when you draw commissary, you buy me a chocolate bar," Duke told the kid.

"Please, please, Duke . . . I don't wanna . . ."

I heard a slap. "Shut up, punk," one of the flunkies said.

"Tomorrow," Duke told the kid. "Or I'll cut your fucking heart out."

Friday, the kid drew his commissary. Handed Duke a chocolate bar. Duke unwrapped it, put it on the radiator. I watched the bar get soft until it flowed down the side of the radiator.

That night, one of the flunkies picked up the gooey bar in the paper in two hands. He carried it, walking next to Duke. Duke went to the kid's bed.

"Give it up," is all he said.

The kid turned over. Duke dropped his pants. Smeared the soft chocolate all over his stiff prick and got on top of the boy.

The boy screamed, once. I heard a squishy sound and then he was quiet.

I was so scared I couldn't cry, like no air was in me.

The Man never came in.

The boy went to the Infirmary the next morning.

It was two weeks later, summer just starting, when Duke told another boy to bring him a chocolate bar the next day. We were chopping weeds on that Friday when the boy who had to bring the chocolate bar, he brought the scythe down over his foot. It went right through. I could see a piece of his toe in the tip of the sneaker.

The Man took him to the Infirmary. They know all about stab wounds there, but they don't keep you long. They took the boy to the hospital, outside the institution.

I thought the boy won then. But they brought him back a few days later, walking on crutches.

The next Friday, Duke walked by the boy's bed. One of his flunkies held up a chocolate bar. Duke smiled at the boy.

"This time, I got my own," he said.

They gang-banged the boy that night. All of them.

The next morning, The Man took him out of the dorm. He never came back.

I thought about it. Every day. Some days, it was all I thought about.

It was just after the 4th of July when Duke and his flunkies came over to me.

"This Friday," he said, "when you draw, buy me a chocolate bar, okay?"

My heart slowed down when he said that. There was a smooth, cold chill inside me. An icy feeling, but it made me warm inside.

I nodded like it was okay. My voice wouldn't work.

Thursday night. I could feel the moon, even if I couldn't see it from my bed. I walked over to it, shining through the window. Duke's bed is just below the window, the best bed in the dorm.

Everybody was asleep. The cottage was full of night sounds, night smells. The Man only looked in when there was noise.

Duke had a big portable radio, the kind with speakers on the side and a tape player and everything. One of his flunkies carried it around for him. I lifted the radio down from the shelf. Big fat batteries inside. I took them out, quiet, quiet.

Duke's sneakers were at the foot of his bed. Brand-new white leather sneakers. His socks were inside, dirty socks from yesterday. One of the boys did his laundry every week for him.

I took out one of the socks. Put the batteries inside the toe. One by one. Soft, so they wouldn't click together.

I held the ankle-part of the sock in my right hand and walked around to the head of the bed in my bare

feet. Where Duke was sleeping on his back. I spread my
legs apart. I could feel wetness on my face but I didn't
make a sound. I swung the sock between his eyes as
hard as I could. His nose splattered, red and white. He
made some moaning sound and rolled over, moving his
hands, but I smashed the sock into the back of his head
again and again. White stuff came out of his head onto
the pillow.

When I stopped, it was all pulp. The sock was sticky
with hair.

I put the sock on the floor, went back to my bed.

They found Duke in the morning. Some men in white
coats came later, with a stretcher. They covered his face
with a sheet.

That night, Friday night, Duke's flunkies walked over to
my bed. One of them was carrying his big radio. They put
it on my bed and walked away.

Later, I turned it on. They'd put new batteries in it for
me.

◆

It was almost five in the morning when I heard a tinkle of
metal against glass. The quarter I'd put on the doorknob
fell off into the ashtray I put on the carpet right under it
—somebody trying the door. I slid off the bed, stood over
to one side. Misty came in, closed the door behind her real
quiet, walked over to the bed.

I said "Ssssh" from behind her—she gave a little jump.

"You *scared* me, honey!"

"It's okay. I didn't know it was you."

"I didn't want to wake you."

"It's okay." I sat down on the chair, watched her as she took off her clothes.

"I got a job," she said. "Dancing. First place I went to, that's good luck, right? I worked a whole shift too." She took some bills out of her purse. "Look, baby. Tips. For only one night. A new girl always does real good."

She handed me the money, the same way the flunky handed me Duke's radio.

♦

In the morning, Misty moved real soft in the bed, pulling off the little blue silk wrapper she was wearing, put her head down between my legs, licking, like she was going to wake me up that way. I shifted my body to let her know I was awake.

She looked up at me from between my legs. "I'll do whatever you want," she said, voice rough and soft.

I closed my eyes. She was a dancer now, Misty. Like the woman I saw in the bar last night, dressed in little-girl clothes. She liked me, Misty. Because I didn't get any nasty fun out of hurting her, the way the hammer did. That was enough for her.

It made me sad.

Shella came into my mind. One night, I came home later than her. She was dressed in a little-girl outfit, like that woman last night. Sat on my lap, made baby noises. I slapped her so hard she fell on the floor, started crying.

It was the first time I hit her, the only time. The only time she ever cried too.

"I only wanted to please you, Daddy," she said. "Men like little girls. I know."

I held her for a long time while she cried then. Promised I'd kill her father for her one day. So she could watch him die.

Thinking about Shella, I grew hard in Misty's mouth.

◆

New York City is a cross-hatch. The streets run east to west, the avenues north to south. The poolroom wasn't more than a couple of miles away. It was a little before ten o'clock when I started out, walking. Misty had gone to her job.

Walking downtown along Eighth Avenue, I saw everything. Cop cars drove past like they didn't.

The poolroom didn't have a sign or anything, but the number was on the door. I opened it, climbed up some metal stairs. It smelled like a housing project.

Upstairs, it was a big room, maybe forty tables. Old-style, all green felt, leather pockets. Sign on one wall. It just said NO in big letters, then little words next to it: Gambling, Foul Language, Alcoholic Beverages, like that.

The place was mostly empty, a dozen tables in use. Just like the prison yard: blacks in one piece of space, whites in another. Spanish, oriental. All separate.

The guy at the desk gave me a plastic tray of balls, pointed to an empty table over in a corner, by the windows.

I carried the tray over to the table, took the balls out one by one. I rolled them around the table with my hand, testing for drag and drift on the felt. The cloth was worn, but it ran true.

I checked the cue sticks racked along the far wall. Numbers are burned into the sticks to tell you the weight.

The highest number was 22. I looked through them until I found one with nice balance, good tip. Put some talc from a dispenser in my left palm, worked the stick through until it slid smooth. Racked the balls, rubbed the cue tip with a little cube of blue chalk I found on the table.

I broke the balls, started sending them home, one by one. It was peaceful there, the table clean and flat, the ivory balls clicking together, going where I sent them.

"You're pretty good," a guy said, coming up behind me like a surprise. I'd seen him when he first started to move. Red-haired guy, light eyes, little scar at the corner of his mouth.

"Thanks," I said.

"You . . . wanna play somebody for somethin'?"

"No thanks. I'm just practicing."

He took a seat on one of the stools, lit a cigarette like he was going to be there for a while. I like the feel of things in my hands. I like making them move, do what I want. When I look close, get locked in, I can see the weave in the felt, the grain of the ivory. The balls look big—I can see the edges where they start to curve. The cue feels like it's coming out of my arm, like a long fingertip. I ran a couple of racks, never looking up. Kiss shots, banks, getting the feel of the rails. I pocketed the last ball, racked them up again, locking the balls against the front of the wooden triangle with my thumbs to make them tight, squaring the angles, getting it perfect. I chalked my cue again, sighting down.

"You calling a shot?" the guy asked me.

"Yes."

"Out of a full rack . . . you *calling* a shot?"

"Yes."

"Which one? Corner ball?"

"Head ball in the side, two rails."

"Twenty says you don't make it."

"It goes about every five times," I told him.

"You want five to one?"

"Okay."

He put a pair of fifties on the table rail. I put down a twenty.

"The five ball?" he asked, making sure. "Five ball in the side?"

"Your side," I said, stepped to the table.

I drove the cue ball past the rack, hard against the back rail, spinning off, cracking into the rack from behind, right between the corner ball and the next one over. The five ball flew toward me, hit the left-hand long rail, banked into the short rail right where I was standing, and dropped into the side pocket like it was ducking out of sight.

"Holy shit!" the guy said. I put the money in my pocket.

He stood there, shaking his head. "You're here to see Monroe, right?"

I swept the balls off the table, put them back into the plastic tray.

"Yes," I said.

◆

He followed me over to the front desk, where I paid for my time on the table. There was a door behind the desk. The red-haired guy knocked, stood there a minute. I heard bolts being turned, and we went inside.

It was a big room, eight-sided poker table in one corner,

four men sitting there. Monroe was at the table, back to the wall.

A thick guy put his hand on my shoulder, like he was going to pat me down.

"Don't bother," Monroe said.

I walked over, stood looking at him.

"Ghost! My man! Haven't seen you in years. You haven't changed a bit, huh?"

"Neither have you," I told him. His black hair was thinner—I could see pale scalp. And his face was heavy, jowly. But I meant what I said.

"Sit down, sit down. You want a drink?"

"A glass of water," I said, sitting down. The guy to Monroe's left laughed. Nobody paid him any attention.

"Man, you should see this guy play, Monroe. Like a fucking machine," the red-haired guy said.

"I've *seen* him play," Monroe said, looking up at the redhead with his little eyes. "You wouldn't like it. Go get him his glass of water."

The redhead went away.

"So what's up, Ghost? This a social call?"

"No," I said, glancing around me. Meaning I didn't want to talk in front of a crowd. Monroe never asked my name —always calls me Ghost. I never asked why.

"Take a walk," Monroe told the others.

I waited a couple of beats. The redhead came back with a glass of water. I thanked him. He didn't say anything, just went away again.

"I'm looking for someone," I told Monroe.

He held up his hands, like he was pushing somebody away. "I don't get involved in other people's business."

"It's not for that," I said. "A woman. My woman. I lost

track of her, last time I was locked up. She's a dancer. I figure, maybe you could ask around, reach out . . . help me find her."

"It's not business?"

"No."

"What'd you have?"

"Her name is Candy. Big girl, late twenties, early thirties. Real light blonde hair, about my height."

He shrugged his shoulders. "A blonde named Candy, dances topless . . . There's a thousand girls fit that description."

"She's got real light eyes, like a gray color. And a little dot, a beauty mark, just over here," I told him, touching the spot on my face. "And a long thin scar, like a wire-mark, on her right thigh, all around the outside."

"What else?"

"She won't turn a trick. She'll B-drink, dry hustle, strip. But she won't sell pussy. Not out of a bar anyway."

"They all will, the right guy comes along."

"She won't have a pimp."

"She's a lesbo?"

"No. I don't know, maybe. . . . It doesn't matter. She won't give her money to anyone else."

"Okay. You know her righteous name?"

"No."

"She got people anywhere?"

"No."

"She could be dead, in jail, whatever. Could be married, have a couple of kids. Those broads, they can't strut the runways forever, you understand?"

"Yes."

He took a long aluminum tube out of his jacket pocket, unscrewed the cap. It was a cigar, wrapped in dark paper.

He clipped off the tip with a little round knife, cracked a wooden match, got it going. "You want this as a favor?" he asked.

"No."

"Same old Ghost. Nothing for nothing, huh?"

"Right."

"So what you got?"

"Money?"

"How much?"

"How much do you want?"

"No money. I *got* money. How about you do what it is you do *for* money . . . for me. One more time."

"Okay."

"Just like that, huh? It don't matter to you?"

"No."

"I'll start tonight, looking. You come back, say, Friday night, same time, okay? Maybe I'll have something for you."

"Thanks."

"And I have your word, right, Ghost? You'll do this other thing for me?"

"Yes."

"It's a deal," he said, leaning forward to shake hands.

◆

Misty got back to the hotel just after I did. She should have been tired from working a shift, but she was all bouncing around, excited.

"I made even more money tonight, baby. It's really good here. We're doing good now, right? Could we, maybe, get an apartment or something? So we didn't have to live in this one room. It's like a prison cell."

"No, it isn't," I told her.

"I didn't mean like *actually*, honey. But, if we have a place of our own, we could have . . . stuff, you know? Our own furniture, maybe. So we could eat a meal inside once in a while, not all this take-out. Could you just *think* about it, okay?"

"I told you, I don't think I'll be staying here long."

"You're leaving?"

"I don't know what I'm doing. But I'll know soon, all right?"

"All right, baby. Whatever you say."

◆

The next couple of days, I stayed inside. Practicing. I can make myself invisible, kind of. Slow down everything inside of me, so slow I can feel the blood move in little streams through my chest. I go somewhere else in my head. Not far, I'm still me. But someplace closed off. Where I don't feel things. It just happened one day, when I was a kid— when they were hurting me. Now I can do it when I want to.

◆

One afternoon, Misty asked me to come to her club.

"I'm on television, honey."

"What?"

"Don't look at me like that—I don't mean like on *real* TV. In the window. It's a new thing. Couldn't you please do it? Just once. I'd really like you to. I mean, you've never seen me . . . work. I'm real good, everybody says so. That's why I'm in the window."

"Is anybody leaning on you?"

"It's not *that*, baby. Please?"

◆

I went the next night. It was just like she said. The club was just a narrow doorway with a little window on one side. They had a TV set suspended from wires hanging there. Black-and-white, like you can rent in cheap rooms. One long loop, the same stuff. Over and over. I stood there and watched until Misty came on. You couldn't tell where she was, like in a dressing room or something. She had a regular dress on. The camera watched her pull it over her head. She had a slip on. She took it off. Then she was in a bra, panties, high heels, and stockings. She kicked off the shoes, unrolled the stockings, bending over with her back to the camera. She unhooked the bra from behind, dropped it on the floor. She was just rolling the panties down over her hips when the tape looped to some other girl.

The barker was a greasy little guy in a blue jacket. He didn't yell and scream like the other ones on the block, just waited for someone to stop and watch the TV, whispered to them.

"They go all the way inside, pal," is what he said to me. "No cover, no minimum."

I went through the door. Dark place, the air stung my eyes. I ordered rum and Coke. Don't mix them, I told the sagging topless waitress. Like I was worried about watered drinks. She gave me a wink like I was a smart guy, knew my way around. I drank a little bit of the Coke, poured the shot of rum into the glass. The waitress came back a little later.

"You don't like the Coke, huh?"

"Just for a little taste," I told her. She brought me another. I did the same thing, left her enough of a tip so she wouldn't make a fuss . . . but not so much that she'd think about working me for more.

A Puerto Rican girl with a blonde wig was on. There was music, but she wasn't really dancing. Just shaking her body parts with the music around her. People threw money on the bar. She'd kneel and pick up the bills. When she got enough, she rolled them all into a little tube, held it up so the watchers could see it, kissed the little roll, stuffed it deep inside her G-string. Every once in a while, she'd pull down the G-string real quick. The money was gone. Inside her, someplace. The men applauded, like she'd done something good.

Misty was different. She really danced, like she was moving to the music. The men didn't clap real loud for her until she got on her hands and knees, crawling the length of the bar, still moving to the music. She took a glass from in front of one man, put one hand inside her G-string, like she was playing with herself, sipped from the glass. Then she poured some of it right on the bar, put her face down, wiggled her butt real hard while she lapped it up. They really cheered for that. Men put money on the bar—Misty crawled over to the ones who put up the most, let them spill their drinks on the bar so she could lap them up again. She crawled off the stage when her number finished, looking back over her shoulder.

◆

When Misty got back, she looked tired. I was watching TV with the sound off, trying to figure out what people were saying from the way they moved. She just said a quick hello, went in the bathroom. I heard the shower.

She came out with a towel around her head, still a little wet.

"Honey?"

"What?"

"I thought you were coming tonight."

"I did."

"I didn't see you."

"I was there."

"Yeah."

"You think I'm lying?"

"I didn't say that, honey. . . . Don't be mad."

"Come here."

She came over to me slowly, her face down. Got on her knees beside the chair. "I'm sorry," she said.

"On the TV screen, in the window, it was black and white, showed you taking off your dress and all. Everything but your pants. Inside, you were dancing to some song . . . 'Fever,' I think it was called. You crawled around on the bar, licking up drinks they spilled."

"You *did* come!"

"Yes. You were very good. Dancer, I mean. Much better than the other ones. You move real nice, like a real dancer."

There were tears on her face. She took the towel off her head, held it in her hands, twisting it like she was trying to get the water out.

"What's the matter?" I asked her.

She put her head in my lap, her hands behind her back. I felt her teeth on the waistband of the pajamas I was wearing. She pulled the string loose, put her mouth on me. I patted the back of her head, sleek from the water. When I got close, I pulled gently back on her hair but she just sucked harder until I went off in her mouth.

◆

Friday night, I went back to the poolroom. They gave me a different table this time. Three tables away, a bunch of Chinese guys were playing, but not really, something else was going on. I watched them the way I watch the TV without the sound. Somebody was buying, somebody was selling. I couldn't tell what.

The red-haired guy came over to my table. "You want to try that shot again?" he asked me.

"No."

"How come? I'll give you the same odds."

"It won't go on this table. The short rail's too stiff."

"So we'll take the table you had before."

"I'm here to see Monroe."

"Yeah, so what? It'll only take a minute."

"I'm here to see Monroe," I told him.

We went through the same door. Monroe was at the table alone this time. I sat down across from him. I could feel the redhead, pushing against a cushion of air just off my left shoulder.

"What?" Monroe said, looking up at him.

"This guy has my money. He hustled me with some trick shot last time he was here. I asked him to do it again, same deal. He wouldn't do it. I should get a chance, get my money back."

"How much did you lose?" Monroe asked him.

"A yard."

Monroe took out a roll of bills, peeled off a hundred, tossed it on the table. "Get lost," he told the redhead.

"I want it from him," the redhead said, not moving.

A crackle in the air, all around me. I could feel watchers, like prison. I didn't move.

Monroe leaned forward. "Don't be stupid," he said.

The redhead was so close I could feel the air from his mouth. "I could do it," he said. "You don't need some outside shooter, do this job. Way I figure it, it's a big contract, this guy's taking my money."

"Go over there and sit down," Monroe said. "I'll talk to you later."

"Hey, come on, Monroe. This guy don't look tough to me."

"Cancer don't *look* tough either. You're out of your league. Now, do what I tell you."

"Hey, fuck you, Monroe."

Monroe looked at me. "You want to fuck this guy up, Ghost? Little favor for me?"

"No."

"You don't do favors for friends?"

"I don't fuck people up."

Monroe started to laugh then, a thin, crazy laugh. It sounded like that glass cracking in my hand. Nobody laughed with him.

"What's so motherfucking funny?" the redhead said.

"You don't get it, do you, kid?"

The redhead backed away, making a triangle out of me and Monroe with him at the tip.

"Get up," he said to me.

I didn't turn around, watching Monroe. "What's the going rate for assholes, Ghost?" he asked me.

"It's the same for anyone," I said.

He laughed again, more juice in it this time. "Okay," he said.

I got up. The redhead was right in my face. He was staring hard. I moved my eyes around his face, getting his picture. His size and shape, the set of his body.

I sat down again. "Okay," I told Monroe.

♦

We went out the back door to a fire escape, climbed metal stairs to the roof. Everybody came up there. One of the other guys brought a metal folding chair. He opened it for Monroe.

City lights all around us, but the roof was dark. Flat, just an electrical shack to one side, big skylight on the other. The door to the shack opened, a man stepped out. It must lead downstairs, be locked from the inside so nobody could burglar the place.

I took off my jacket. I was wearing a sweatshirt. Extra-large. It was baggy on me, loose and comfortable. I pulled it up to my neck, taking the T-shirt with it, holding it like that so they could see I didn't have a gun. I walked around a few feet, feeling the roof under the thin soles of my gym shoes.

The redhead took out a knife. A big one, brass knuckles around the handle, little teeth along the top edge of the blade.

One of Monroe's guys stepped forward, a short piece of rope in his hand.

"You want to rope dance?" Monroe asked the redhead.

"No, fuck that. Just give him a blade—let's get it on."

The guy stepped back. Everybody took out money, whispering in the black corners.

"Okay?" Monroe asked the redhead.

"Yeah. Do it!"

Monroe nodded. "You okay, Ghost?"

I nodded, watching the redhead. He came in like a crab, in a crouch, the knife in his right hand, holding it underhand, blade facing in. He took a swipe—I stepped to one side, watching. He was making a noise to himself, like a hum from a generator. Each time he came in, swiped, stepped back. Closing the line, coming nearer every time. I moved my left hand to my right wrist, slid back the cuff to the sweatshirt, let the car antenna slide into my hand. I snapped my wrist and it came out, telescoping to about five feet. I whipped it across his left hand before he saw what it was. He made a noise as I brought it around in a stream, slashing an X across his face. His hands came up, blood sprayed around them, and the knife fell. I kicked it away, moved in on him, giving him time, pulling the cuff off my left wrist. He grabbed for the antenna. I let him take it, raking the sharpened can opener I had taped to my left wrist across his face. I locked it in deep, pulling against the muscles. It caught near his mouth as he hit the ground, me on top. I pulled it free. He was screaming then. I chopped at the side of his neck until I felt it go.

I used the front of his shirt to wipe off the can opener and the antenna. I could smell where one of the guys had thrown up on the roof.

We all went downstairs. Some of the guys paid money to Monroe. I saw the money on the table. Monroe separated some of it, gave it to me. He saw I was looking at the money that was left.

"That's the difference between you and me, Ghost," he said. "Don't ever forget it."

I didn't say anything.

Monroe told me not to come back there. He gave me a place to meet him in two nights. Told me the car he'd be in.

◆

I went out the next afternoon, bought the papers. There was nothing about finding a body on a roof.

I don't read much. Just the papers once in a while. To see if there's trouble. Shella used to read to me, sometimes. It started when I got hurt. This guy was coming to watch Shella dance every night. He asked her for a date—she told him she didn't date the customers. So he started calling her at work. The first couple of times, she took the calls. He scared her, with those calls. That's hard to do to Shella, but he did it. Kept saying, if she wasn't going to give him a piece of ass, he was going to take one for himself. Cut it off her one night. Told her he had a razor. I told her the guy was playing with himself, talking to her like that, getting off on her being scared. I tried to tell her how I knew, from listening to guys like him the last time I was locked up. Freaks, I know them. You just listen, they'll tell you everything. He never came back to the club. I told Shella, just don't talk to him on the phone, he'll find someone else to give his terror to. She promised me. But she lied. I always knew when Shella lied.

He was waiting for her, one night. In the alley behind the club, where she walked through to get to the car. A shortcut. I was there too. Every night, I was there. Ever since I found out she was lying.

He didn't know what he was doing, the freak. When Shella came through the mouth of the alley, he was breathing so loud I could hear him from where I was waiting. You couldn't miss Shella, clicking in her high heels, white-blonde hair piled up on her head. Alone.

The freak knocked some garbage cans together when he got to his feet. Shella didn't run. Stupid bitch, Shella. She stopped, pulled something out of her purse. I could see the red neon glitter on the metal.

"Come on, cocksucker!" she yelled at the freak. "Come and get it. I got one too."

He stepped out of the shadows. It looked like he had only one arm, the sleeve of his coat dangling empty. Nothing in his other hand. He staggered like he was drunk, mumbling like he was scared Shella was a crazy woman, going to hurt him for nothing. She made a disgusted noise, snorting through her nose. She only saw a crippled drunk, trying to find a quiet place to sleep. Dropped the razor back in her purse, spun around, and started to walk out of the alley. He flew at her like a giant bat, coat flapping around him. The angle was wrong—I had too much ground to cover. He almost had her from behind when I kicked his knees from the side. He went down against the wall, came back up fast. I went at him from the empty-sleeve side—felt the flash of something heavy coming at me, threw up my hand—the lead pipe cracked across the side of my hand, right into my face. I didn't feel it until after I was done with him.

Shella got me into the car, took me to the room. My left eye was closed, my nose was all flat, pushed to one side. It bled a lot.

We couldn't go to a hospital. Shella got ice from the ice machine in the hall, wrapped it in a towel, smashed it with

the lead pipe. I pushed my nose back where it should be
with my fingers and Shella put the towel with the crushed
ice over my face, like a mask. She gave me some Percodan
she had, and I got woozy—I'm not used to drugs.

The lead pipe had tape all around one end, for a better
grip. In the freak's wallet, we found the number to the pay
phone at the club.

I was lying on the bed, on my back. We'd have to stay
a while now. If Shella left the same night the cops found
the freak in the alley, if they stopped the car somewhere
and saw my face . . .

She came over to the bed, carrying a chair in one hand,
sat down next to me.

"You should whip my ass," she said.

I didn't say anything.

"This is my fault. I didn't listen to you. I was talking to
him on the phone, every time he called. Told him he better
leave me the fuck alone, I wasn't playing. I thought he'd
run away, I talked to him like that. But it made him mad.
I didn't want to tell you . . . what I did . . . so I decided
I'd deal with him myself. Phone freaks, they never show
up in person. Like flashers. I was on the train once, in
Chicago. Late at night. This guy opens his coat and it's all
hanging out. He's hard and all, getting off on it. I ran over
and grabbed him, right by the root. Almost yanked it off,
the motherfucker. I thought . . . I'm sorry, baby."

"It's okay," I told her. Tired, not sleepy.

"You want me to . . . ?" she asked, trailing her fingers
along my cock. It was soft, small.

"No."

She gave me a little kiss on my chest. Got up and went
somewhere.

When she came back, I was the same way. I could feel

her sit in the chair next to the bed. "Would you like me to read to you, honey?"

I said "Sure." I don't know why I said that.

It was one of those romance books she was always reading. Paperbacks. I listened to her read, watched the story in my head. It was a stupid story, something about a princess. Her father wanted her to marry the son of some other king, make some political deal. She ran away. She got captured by some pirates. They had her tied up in a chair when the pirate captain came in. She started giving him orders when I fell asleep.

Shella fed me hot soup the next morning. Washed my face with a hot towel, gave me another Percodan, made another ice mask for me. I laid down, resting. She asked me, did I want her to read to me some more.

I told her okay.

She went to work that night. She said, if the cops took her, she wouldn't tell them where she lived. If she didn't come back, I should figure she was locked up.

She came back, though. Said the cops didn't even question the girls in the club.

Shella got a bunch of different books. She'd get them at the drugstore, off the racks. All kinds. She read to me every morning, every night when she got back to the room.

I got better every day.

One night, she asked me what was my favorite. Of all the books she read to me.

I didn't like the sex books. Or the westerns. The mysteries, like with clues, they were too complicated, too silly. I thought about it. The Sherlock Holmes stories, I told her. When she asked me why, I told her because the stories were short. When she was at work, I thought about it. Why

I liked those stories. They were so close, always together, Holmes and that doctor. Watson. Friends to the end. Real partners. Even when Watson got married, he was with Holmes. Holmes, he was ice-cold. Always did the smart thing, figured stuff out. But in one story, I forget the name, he told some guy, if anything had happened to Watson, the guy was dead.

There was lots and lots of those stories. Some were longer, like books.

Shella read to me all the time when I was getting better. Even after we left that town, when my face was healed, she would read to me sometimes. Like a treat.

There were still plenty of the Sherlock Holmes stories left when I went down in Florida.

◆

I met Monroe a little after midnight. He gave me the address: Pike Slip, off South Street. It was under a big highway on the East Side, slab of concrete like a parking lot, but no cars came there. He was in a black limo, like he was coming from a party. I saw it pull in from where I was watching. The glass in the back windows was black like the car.

I stepped out so they could see me. The back window came down. I walked over.

"Get in, Ghost," Monroe said.

Inside, it was like a living room. All leather, even a wood bar that came down from the back of the front seat. Just Monroe in the back seat. I could see two men in the front, sitting behind a screen, facing front.

"You ready to work?" he asked me.

"Yes."

"I'm a businessman, okay? I got a lot of business. There's this guy, Carlos. Carlos the Colombian, they call him. He don't know how to do things—he's a fucking animal."

I don't care why people do things. Everybody's got a reason—it doesn't change anything, why they do it. But I didn't tell Monroe that. I learned, from doing this a long time, I learned not to say anything. I just let people talk until they tell me what I need. Sometimes I nod, like I'm listening.

"We told this fucking guy, we told him he can't move weight in this town without the say-so. He's got prime stuff, I'll give him that. All we wanted was a taste, just a slice off the top. I told him nice, there's plenty for everyone, don't be greedy, you know?"

That's when I nodded. So he'd finish.

"He fucks with his own product, thinks he's Superman, nobody can take him down. Goes everywhere with this fucking army. Way I heard it, he's got himself a deal. With the *federales*. Walks around like he's got immunity. Never gets busted. Anyway, you can't get to him where he lives. Wherever the fuck *that* is, someplace out in Queens, Jackson Heights. Chapinero, they call it. Spanish for something, maybe their home town. It's all Spanish out there, wall to wall. You speak any Spanish?"

"No."

"Anyway, it ain't the money, Ghost. Everybody's got a boss. Even me, I got to answer to people. I've been paying the slice myself. For a couple a months now. You understand what I'm saying? I slice his action off the top, they slice mine. They don't care how I get it, I got to get it. They know he's moving weight, they expect me to slice it.

I tell them I can't move on this guy, they move on me. That's the way it works, right?"

I nodded again.

"Only place he goes, only place we know, is this club. Over there, in this Chapinero. Looks like a storefront on the street, but the whole cellar, they use it for this club. He goes there alone, goes downstairs alone, anyway. Leaves his boys upstairs. He likes to dance, down there. Brings a broad with him, puts on a show. I got people, watch him. He don't carry a piece.

"I send two shooters down there, couple of weeks ago. Another guy for backup. The two shooters get dead. The guy who comes out, he tells us, the place is all dark, little spotlights on the dance floor, that's all. This Carlos, he's dancing with some cunt, got his hands all over her. The shooters roll on him, bang-bang, they both get dead. The other guy, he didn't see the whole thing, but when the lights come on, Carlos, he's just standing there, nothing in his hands. Turns out they was shot in the chest, head-on. Like it happened by itself. No way Carlos does it, not like that."

Monroe's face looks at me. Just his face, not his eyes. "You got nothing to say?" he asks me.

"No."

"You understand what I'm telling you? He shoots people without a gun, okay?"

"Okay."

"This is the guy you got to do, Ghost. Here's a picture of him. You do this, I'll find this broad, Candy. I'll hunt her down for you." He looks at me with his eyes now. "We got a deal?"

"Yes," I told him.

♦

When Misty got home, I asked her, does she have to work every night.

"I don't *have* to, baby. I mean, I could have a night off anytime, I guess, I just ask the boss."

"Do you want to go someplace with me? A nightclub, like?"

"Sure! I love to party, honey. I didn't think you . . . Where would you like to go?"

"This club I heard about. In Queens. It's supposed to be nice."

"Can we go tonight?"

"Next week," I told her.

♦

I took a train to the neighborhood the next day. When I bought the token for the subway, the lady gave me a map, different-colored lines, all the stops on there. It started out underground, but then it went outside. I got out, walked around. Like Monroe said, the whole neighborhood was Spanish—the restaurants, the drugstores, even the news-papers. I walked by the storefront. It looked closed in the daytime, the window was painted over. I could read the neon sign, even when it wasn't lit. Bajo Mundo.

I couldn't see if there was a back way out. People wouldn't come to a nightclub on the subway, but I couldn't see a parking lot either.

I walked around a little bit more. I wasn't worried about people getting a look at me. Nobody sees me.

♦

I went back the next night. The elevated-train platform looks down on the club. I stood there, looking down. Cars drove up. Fancy, sleek cars. A couple of guys out front, they would take each car, drive it off somewhere. Somewhere off the block—I couldn't see where they went. Like at a country club.

I was counting the cars, trying to figure out how big the place was inside. It was about ten o'clock. The man I was looking for, I couldn't see him. Maybe he didn't come until late.

I felt them come up behind me, but I kept watching, over the railing. When they got close, one said something in Spanish. I turned around. The guy who was talking, he had a gun. They were wearing those sweatshirts with hoods on them. I was all the way at the end of the platform, dark there. Other people maybe a hundred feet away. I knew they wouldn't do anything.

I put my hands up. The guy without the gun, he reached in my jacket pocket, took out my wallet. There was maybe three hundred bucks in there. He took it. The guy with the gun made a motion like I should turn around. I did that.

I heard them move away. One of them said something. Marry-con, it sounded like.

♦

Just before midnight, three cars pulled in together. The man I was watching for got out of the back seat from the middle car. He looked just like the picture Monroe showed me. The man held out his hand, and a woman took it, came out after him. They went into the club. Men got out of the other cars, stood by the door.

When other cars pulled up, those men watched.

Just before three o'clock, the same three cars pulled up in front. The man came out, the woman just in front of him. All three cars pulled away in a line.

◆

I got my car out of the garage at the hotel the next afternoon, drove over to the neighborhood. I just drove around for a while until I found a parking space a couple of blocks away from the club. I read the signs. The car wouldn't get a ticket even if it was there for a couple of days. I left it there, took the train back.

◆

I was awake when Misty came back. I smoked a cigarette while she took her shower. She came out, wearing a pink silk thing that sort of wrapped around her.

"Do you like this?" she asked me.

"It's pretty."

She did a spin so I could see the whole thing. Sat down on the bed. Stretched like she was real tired from work.

I laid down on the bed next to her, looking at the ceiling.

"Can you get credit cards?" I asked her.

"Sure, honey. Someone's always looking to sell them at the club. What kind?"

"American Express, Mastercard, Visa . . . any big card."

"Fresh ones go for a yard. And they're only good for a couple-three days. You know . . . ?"

"Yeah." You can always get credit cards. They rough them off in purse-snatchings, slip them out of pocketbooks in the ladies' rooms . . . then they sell them. Most people use them to buy things. Then they sell the things. To the same kind of people they stole the cards from.

"You have a driver's license?"

"No, baby. I mean, I got ID, but . . ."

"It's okay."

She rolled against me, put her head on my chest, reached down, started playing with me.

"What do you need, honey? Tell Misty, I'll get it for you."

"We need a car. For when we go to this club. A fancy, nice car. We're going to rent a car, leave it there, understand? Go home in our own car."

"Why don't we just take a limo?"

"A limo?"

"Sure! We can rent one. Just for the night, okay? It doesn't cost that much. Like a taxi, only fancy. Some of the guys, the ones who come to the club, they use them. When they're ready to leave, they just make a call, the car's waiting for them out front."

"They're like cabs, right? They have a log, write down where they take people?"

"I . . . guess so."

"No good."

SHELLA

♦

I thought about it, turned it over in my mind. I don't do things fast, except when I get right to them. Shella wasn't like that, always impatient. She was always playing, not thinking how things would come out.

We had some money ahead, once, and she wanted to rent this little house, like a cottage, right near the beach. It was okay with me. Neither of us was working then. A vacation, she said it was. Nighttime, I would go out to the beach, look at the dark water. Sometimes she came with me. One night, she didn't. When I walked back to the house, I saw the car was gone, no lights on. Figured she went into town—Shella got restless sometimes. I opened the front door, felt somebody there. I slid back out the door, closed it softly, didn't click the latch. I went around the back of the house . . . couldn't find where anybody'd got in. I found a good spot, where I could see the car when she came in. Whoever was inside, they'd have to come out sometime.

The car pulled up a couple of hours later. The door opened and I could see someone inside. Not Shella. Small, dark-haired. Whoever it was closed the door, started for the house. I stepped behind him, locked my forearm around his throat, kicked his ankles, took him down. I smelled perfume, felt long hair. A woman.

"Make a sound, I'll break your neck," I said, quiet. "Who's inside?"

"Candy," she whispered. "She lent me the car. Don't . . ."

"Who are you?"

"Bonnie. Her friend, Bonnie."

"You work at the club?" Her body was slim, slender like a boy's. Whatever she was, she was no dancer.

"Upstairs. I work the phones. Please don't hurt me."

"Where'd you get the car?"

"Candy lent it to me."

"When?"

"Nine o'clock. She brought it out to me. I told her I'd have it back by midnight—she's gonna drive me home."

"It's after midnight."

"I know. She's gonna beat my ass."

I didn't get it when she said it. I walked her over to the front door. "It's open," I told her. "Just walk in, call her name. If she's in there, by herself, there's no problem."

I touched a spot where her neck met her shoulder, felt her jump with the pain. "Don't try to run," I told her.

She opened the door. I heard her call "Candy?" I waited outside.

◆

A light came on in the house. Then another. I went around to the back, slipped in a window. I heard a sound from the front. Flesh on flesh. The girl Bonnie was on her knees. Shella was slapping her with one hand, holding the girl's hair in the other. I stepped forward, let Shella see me.

"What?" I asked her.

"It's okay. This bitch was late, that's all," Shella said to me. She turned her head, looked at the girl. "Weren't you?" she said. Slapped her again, hard.

"I thought—"

"It's okay," she said to me. Again. "I'm taking her home."

Shella was dressed all in black, like a bodysuit. Boots on her feet, face all made up like she was going out. "We'll finish this later."

I didn't know who she was talking to when she said that.

They went out together. I heard the car start up.

◆

Shella didn't come back until the next afternoon. I was in the front room, watching television.

"How come you never put the sound on?" she asked me.

"I'm trying to learn how to read lips."

She gave me a funny look, said she was going to take a shower.

When she came back inside, I was still there.

"You never ask questions, do you?"

"Sometimes."

"What you saw, last night. It's just a game, okay?"

"Sure."

"I do that, sometimes."

"All right."

"You don't care?"

"I don't know what it is."

She sat on the arm of my chair, smelling like soap and powder. "You want me to do something for you?"

I closed my eyes. Felt so tired.

"Want me to read to you, baby? Read you a book?"

I nodded, thinking about it. She gave me a little kiss, a sweet kiss.

When I woke up, it was dark. A blanket over me. Shella was gone.

♦

I knew there was something in the memory. I didn't push it, just let it pass through me. Like pain. I can see the inside of my body, sometimes. I got shot, once. A little gun. Just above the knee. It went in and out. I could see the hole in my pants when I took them off. In and out. I could see the path of the bullet. Like a tunnel, all red and clotted with white stuff. I wrapped a bandage around it, real tight. I saw inside my leg, saw the tunnel close, fill up. It got better. The scars are like dots, front and back.

Memory. Shella slapping that girl. A hotel room. In Huntsville, Alabama. Some convention. Shella said we could make some heavy scores. When we checked in, I saw the signs for the convention. Women Executives. Advertising or something. I gave Shella a look. She winked at me. Told me we wouldn't work Badger—she'd get the money herself. Just be ready if something went bad.

I was in the connecting room when I heard her come in. I heard voices, then the sound of a belt. Shella wouldn't turn hard tricks. I looked through the door. A fat woman was on the bed, face down, her wrists and ankles tied to the bedposts, a pillowcase over her head. Shella was whipping her. The back of the fat woman's thighs were red against her pale-white skin.

Shella showed me the money later. A lot of money. Why was Shella whipping that woman staying in my mind? I never remember anything for nothing. I let it run, waiting.

I got it. When Shella worked that convention, we had another room. In a motel out on the highway. Took a cab to the convention hotel when we checked in. Like we were coming from the airport. When we checked out of the hotel, we took a cab to the airport. Then we caught another one back to the motel, where we had our car.

◆

When Misty got back, I told her I knew how to do it. Told her we'd go next Friday night. She ran over, gave me a big kiss like I'd done something great.

◆

The phone rang in the hotel room. It never rings. Nobody has the number. I pointed at Misty—she picked it up.

"Oh! I'll be right down. No, wait a minute. Can you send someone up with them? Okay. Thanks." She bustled around the room, pulling on a pair of slacks.

"What?"

"You'll see, baby."

A knock at the door. Friendly knock. Misty opened it. A bellboy in a uniform, whole mess of packages on one of those carts they use in hotels to move luggage. The bellboy put the stuff where Misty pointed, on the bed. He never looked at me. Misty gave him some bills. He sort of bowed, saying thanks. It must of been too much money.

When he closed the door, Misty locked it, put on the chain. Danced around, flinging off her clothes.

She opened one of the packages, opened another. Took out a little red piece of leather, held it up.

"Isn't it beautiful?"

"What is it?"

"A *dress*, baby. Wait . . . see, it goes with these shoes, and I have stockings for it, and . . ."

"How come . . .?"

She was looking at the dress—I could see it was a dress, now that she told me—holding it up. "I'll have to use powder to get this on, but wait'll you see . . ."

She ran off into the bathroom. Closed the door. She doesn't usually do that, close the door. I heard the shower. Turned on the TV.

When she came out, she was in the red dress. It was so tight, she had to take little steps. The top of the dress pushed her breasts together so hard they were popping out over the red leather. Big zipper right down the front. The skirt was way up on her thighs. She had black stockings, red spike heels the same color as the dress. Her arms and her neck were bare, hair pulled up on top of her head, long earrings, little red balls at the end, dangling.

"What do you think?"

"It's beautiful," I told her. Shella had pranced around like that once, asked me how she looked. I told her "Good" and she threw an ashtray at me. So I knew not to say that again.

"See how it shows me off, honey? With these heels, and the dark stockings . . . ? Like I have long legs, yes?"

"Yes."

"I don't know how I'm gonna sit down in this. And I can't wear pants under it either. But it's worth it. I mean, I want you to be proud of me when we go out."

"I am proud of you. You look great, Misty."

"For real?"

"I swear."

"Wait'll you see the best part!" she said, rooting around in the other packages.

I watched her bending over the bed. The skirt rode up, white flesh above the thick black bands at the top of her stockings. I could see her sex.

"Look!" she said, holding up some black clothing.

"What is it?"

"It's a *suit*, honey. For you. You don't have clothes for a nightclub."

I let her fuss with the stuff. She was right—I never thought of it. A black suit. Smooth, shiny. A white shirt, like they wear with tuxedos, all ruffles in front. The shirt had little black buttons, black cufflinks. She even had black boots. Alligator, they looked like.

"Everything fits," I said. Surprised.

"I measured you, honey. In your sleep. Every square inch. Do you like it?"

"It's great," I said, letting her close all the little snaps and buttons on the shirt. I got into the pants. The waist was fine, but they didn't feel right. "They're too tight," I said.

"No, they're not. Here . . ." She opened the snap at the top, moved around behind me, reached inside my underwear, grabbed my cock, moved it to one side. "Try them now."

They closed fine. I gave her a look. "That means you carry left, honey. You don't . . . I mean, it's not supposed to be right in the *middle*, you understand? Once you put it where it's supposed to be, it won't move, okay?"

She looked so young then. Like something mattered, so much. I felt Shella near me, nudging me in the ribs, rolling her eyes like she did when she said I was being stupid. "It won't stay like this, I see you in that dress," I told Misty. Her face lit up.

The jacket fit real good. I looked at myself in the mirror. "The shoulders are too big," I told Misty. They stuck way out.

"They're *supposed* to be like that," she said. "It's the fashion."

◆

Later, I was on my back, Misty on top of me, breasts just brushing my face. Inside her, feeling her hard muscles inside the soft flesh. She was wet, dripping on me, pumping.

When she was done, she fell asleep like that.

◆

Later again, she woke up. Rolled off me, lit a cigarette. Put her head against her shoulder, blew smoke at the ceiling.

"How did I look in that dress, honey?"

"Beautiful."

"You *said* that. That's not what I mean. Did you think I looked like a . . . what? A college girl?"

"No."

"A whore, then?"

"No. Not that."

"But . . . what, baby?"

I took a hit off her cigarette, thinking for the truth. "What do you call those things you dance in?"

"Costumes?"

"No. The G-string, like. The little strap that goes between your cheeks."

"That *is* a G-string."

"No. What do you call the thicker ones, like with a panel in front?"

"Oh!" She jumped off the bed, looked through the drawers in the fake-wood bureau against the wall. "This?" she asked, holding up a piece of black silk.

"I don't know. . . ."

She climbed into it, showed me. From the front, it looked like a pair of panties, but there was nothing covering the side of her legs, nothing behind but the strip that divided her butt.

"Turn around," I told her. "Bend over."

When she did, it was like she was naked, but her sex was covered by the black cloth.

"What do you call that?"

"A thong, honey."

"Can you get one the same color as the dress?"

"Sure! That's a *good* idea. I shoulda thought of it. You're so sweet. It's . . . prettier that way, huh?"

"Yes."

◆

"Are we going to dance, baby? At the club?" It was the next morning, way before she had to go to work.

"I don't know how," I told her. I hadn't thought about it.

"Didn't you ever learn?"

"No."

"Want me to teach you?"

"It wouldn't do any good," I told her. Thinking of Shella. How she tried to show me. "Just hold me, one hand on my shoulder . . . like that . . . yes . . . one hand on my waist, okay? Now just move with the music—I'll follow you." It didn't work. I tried and tried—I never get tired—but it didn't work. I kept bumping her, pushing her around, stepping on her feet. Shella finally quit. "I don't get it," she said. "I've watched you snatch flies out of the air without even hurting them. You move so beautiful when you're . . . working. But . . . it's like there's no music in you." I shook my head. Misty came over to me, smiling.

"Come on, let's just try, okay?"

I went along with it. Some song playing on the radio. It was no good. Finally, Misty just put her head against my chest, stood there close to me, swaying a little until the song was over.

◆

Friday afternoon, we took off. Misty had made a reservation at one of the motels near the airport. LaGuardia Airport, only a few miles from where we had to go later. The cab dropped us right in front, like we came in on a plane.

The room was the same as all of them. Misty took a shower for a long time. I watched TV. Then she made a call, to have the limo come for us at ten o'clock that night. She laid out everything on the bureau: makeup, nail polish, hair brushes. She said she was going to take a nap, to wake her at seven so she could get ready.

I thought it through while she was asleep. It didn't have to be tonight. Maybe he wouldn't even be there.

◆

We stood out in front of the motel, waiting so the limo driver wouldn't have to call up to the room. The parking lot was full of people making deals, standing around in little groups, talking through the windows of cars. They weren't slick about it. I saw a car pull up, three guys walk over to it. Two other guys got out of the back, opened the trunk. One guy looked through the trunk, took out a flat suitcase, opened it up, looked inside. They traded the suitcase for an airline bag, and the car drove off.

Men walked by, looked at Misty. She held on to my arm, just a light touch. Two men came up the steps, all dressed up in peacock clothes. One of them smiled at Misty, said something in Spanish. The other looked at me real hard. I dropped my eyes. I could smell their perfume as they went past us, laughing.

The limo was on time. The driver had a business suit on, wearing a cap with a little peak. He opened the back door, held it for Misty. We climbed inside.

Once we got rolling, Misty told him we changed our minds, gave him the address of the club, not someplace in Manhattan, where she'd told them at first. He looked over his shoulder, said he was sorry, but it would have to be the same price. Misty told him it was okay.

The cops ask him any questions, all he'd ever remember was Misty busting out of that dress. Me, I look like anybody.

The limo pulled right in front of the club. The driver came around the curb side. I got out first, held out my hand to Misty. Just the way he did, when I was watching him from up on the train platform.

I gave the driver a twenty. Misty told him we'd call his dispatcher when we were ready to come home.

The two bodyguards out front never looked at us.

Inside the door, a man was sitting at a white table, a gray metal box in front of him. I gave him a hundred, he handed me back a fifty. A short, muscular guy was standing next to the table. He tilted his head, and we followed the directions. There was another room straight ahead. I stood still while a skinny guy ran his hands over me. He wasn't playing around, checked my ankles, inside of my thighs, small of my back. He had a knife in a shoulder holster—I never saw one like that before.

A woman was there too—looked like a jailhouse matron, short hair, heavy forearms. She ran her hands over Misty, looked in her purse.

We kept walking, following some people in front of us. Staircase leading down. I went first, feeling Misty's hand on my shoulder.

We found a table against one wall. The place was dark, soft blue lights running in thin tubes all around the ceiling. A waitress came over, wearing a short black dress with a white apron in front. Misty ordered a frozen Daiquiri, I ordered rum and Coke, two glasses.

The room was laid out in a crooked circle, tables all around the sides. In the center, there was a dance floor. The music was slow, stringy stuff . . . guitars and piano. I couldn't see a band, the music came from everywhere. Finally, I spotted a few of the speakers—there must've been dozens of them.

A couple of tables away, a tall woman with a wild mane of black hair took out a mirror, tapped some coke onto it from a silver tube, chopped it into lines, snorted a line into each nostril through a rolled-up bill. Then she passed the mirror to the man with her.

When people went on the dance floor, baby spotlights shot down from the ceiling. Off and on, little pools of white light, big puddles of black. Like prison searchlights, just roaming around, nobody at the controls.

I drank some of the Coke, poured the shot glass of rum into what was left. When the waitress came, we ordered the same again.

After a while, we got up to dance. Just stood on the edge of the dance floor, not moving. Misty rubbed against me. I put my head down so I could hear what she was saying, but she was just singing some song to herself.

◆

He came in just before midnight. With the same woman. They took him to a table that stood off by itself. Nothing else was close to it.

I couldn't be sure it was him, this Carlos that Monroe told me about, until he got up to dance. A tall, narrow man, black hair pulled straight back from his forehead, tied in the back with a ponytail. He was wearing a long white coat, like cowboys wear, only silk. When he stood up, it was almost down to his ankles. The woman with him was wearing pants made out of that stretch stuff, like they wear for exercising, so tight her rear was two separate halves. The pants were black around the calves but they got lighter and lighter as they went up. The part covering her butt was silver. He held the coat open and she stepped inside, dancing by herself while he stood there. His hands were covered with diamonds—he held them so they framed her butt, silver wiggling inside the flash. Her hands were around his waist—I couldn't see them under the long coat.

When they sat down, a waitress brought him a silver tray, little mound of white powder on it. The woman with him had a tiny spoon on a chain around her neck. She sat on his lap, scooped some powder, held it to his nose. Did it again. She didn't take any for herself.

◆

A heavyset man came in with a blonde on his arm. The blonde was in an orange dress cut all the way down to her waist, held together with straps across the front. Misty leaned over to me. "You think I look like that?" she asked.

I wasn't sure what to say, so I shook my head.

"She looks like a cheap piece of goods," Misty said. "No class."

I nodded, watching the woman on the man's lap.

Carlos and the woman got up to dance again. The music was faster now, but Carlos still didn't move. The woman was climbing all over him, twisting like a snake, working hard.

"What's that dance, that they're doing?" I asked Misty.

"It's the Lambada . . . or, anyway, it's *supposed* to be. That skinny bitch can't shake it worth a damn. You see the way those pants are cut . . . to make her look like she's got a decent butt? She wouldn't last ten minutes on a runway."

The woman's legs were all hard muscle under the pants. I still couldn't see her hands.

◆

Misty got up to go to the ladies' room. When she came back, she told me all about it. Gold trim around the mirrors, a maid with towels, trays of perfume, coke.

The later it got, the more crowded it was. The smoke was so heavy it stung my eyes. Misty was used to it, she said it wasn't so bad.

I got up to dance with Misty again. We moved closer to Carlos. I watched him over Misty's shoulder. His eyes were closed.

In between dances with the woman, he hit the spoon again and again. The woman never got up by herself, never went to the ladies' room, never left his side.

I figured it out, finally.

◆

I pulled Misty's chair right against mine, put my arm around her, moved her close so I could whisper to her.

"I'm going to do my work soon," I told her. "Walk out, like we had a fight or something. Get them to call you a cab. Go back to the motel, check out. Take a cab back home."

"What're you . . . ?"

"Ssssh, Misty. Just do it, okay?"

"Baby, couldn't I . . . help you or something?"

Her bare shoulder was warm under my hand. I rubbed her flesh with my thumb, making a little circle.

"Is there a window in the ladies' room?"

"I don't know, honey. I mean, I didn't see one. But I could go and look. . . ."

"Yeah. Do that, okay. I'm going to take a look around myself."

She went off. I gave her a couple of minutes. Then I walked across the dance floor, found the corridor to the men's room, went inside.

It was fancy, like Misty described. But you could see it had been a corner of the basement, once. Maybe there'd been a restaurant upstairs. I went into one of the stalls, last one on the end, near the wall. Pipes running all around the base of the wall. I saw a paper tag wired to one of the pipes. Brooklyn Union Gas, it said.

I came out of the stall, washed my hands, looked in the mirror so I could see the place. In one corner, two pipes running floor-to-ceiling. On the side of the pipes, a round valve. For the kitchen that used to be upstairs?

I got back to the table before Misty did. She sat down, waited till the waitress brought us some more drinks. "There's a window, baby. But it's a real little one, with bars on the outside."

"It's okay. People watch you real close in there? Could you maybe do something before you leave?"

"Honey, I could do *anything*. . . . It's like an orgy room back there. They're all snorting up, making a mess. I saw two girls going at it in one of the stalls, right in front of everybody. This one girl was standing on the toilet with her dress up and the other one was lapping it up. They didn't even close the door."

"Yeah, they're doing it at the tables too."

"Not coke, baby, sex. This one girl was standing on the toilet with her dress all the way up and this other one was eating her. It was disgusting. . . ."

"Okay." I handed her three books of paper matches. "Put a lighted cigarette in the matches, like this." I showed her.

When the cigarette burned down, it would hit the match heads, make a little flash flame. Shella taught me that trick. "Is there a trash can, for tissues and stuff like that?"

"Yeah. There's a couple of them."

"You think you could throw a lighted cigarette in there, wrap the matchbooks around it first?"

"Sure."

We got up to dance again. The floor was so crowded now, people kept bumping into us—especially Misty. I put my lips real close to her ear, holding her tight.

"When we go back to the table, you just sit there and wait. When I come back, you go to the ladies' room, do what we said. Soon as you dump the cigarette, walk right upstairs and step out on the sidewalk. Like you need some air. Grab a cab."

"What're you . . . ?"

"I'll see you later, okay?"

She pulled my face down, gave me a deep kiss.

◆

It took me a while to work my way through the crowd to the men's room. I waited till it was pretty empty. Waited some more until I was alone. Then I stepped out of the stall. The attendant was cleaning up near the door. I stepped over to the pipes, grabbed the valve, and twisted hard. It wouldn't move. I pulled in a deep breath through my nose, got a better grip, then let it out as I twisted it again. I felt little pinpricks in the back of my neck, pain around my eyes . . . felt the valve give. I twisted it open all the way, heard a little hiss.

I went back outside. Misty got up, rubbing her head like it hurt. She went off.

I smoked two cigarettes, slow and easy. It was about fifteen minutes before I smelled it, just a faint undertrace, but I knew what it was. Couldn't move yet. Carlos was still sitting down.

Finally, he got up to dance. I got up too, started across the floor. The woman was wiggling against him, hands behind his back. I heard someone say "Gas?" I guess it's the same in Spanish. People were moving around, the music was loud. . . . Some of them could smell it.

I stepped behind the woman, hooked her as hard as I could in the kidneys. The blow knocked her into him. He spread his arms and she went down, crumpled. I could see the gun in her hand, but she was gone. His mouth was open. Somebody screamed. I shot a left into his ribs, my right hand knife-edged against his neck as his head came down. The gas smell was strong now. "Fire!" I heard someone yell. Everybody started running for the exit, a crazed crowd, stomping over each other.

I got out in the middle of the mess, running. Found the car where I left it.

◆

When I got back to the hotel, Misty was already there. Still in the red dress. She hugged me real tight, told me she got out of the club without any problem. The TV was on. She'd been watching the news. There was nothing.

I took off my clothes, took a shower. When I came out, she was still in the red dress.

"I wanted to keep it on, baby. It looks so pretty, doesn't it?"

"It looks perfect," I told her.

Early in the morning, just before she fell asleep, Misty

moved against me. "Will I ever get to wear my dress again, honey?"

"Sure," I said, holding her till she nodded off.

♦

In the papers the next morning, they just called it a gas leak in the social club. One unidentified dead man, broken neck. And a woman, broken ribs and internal injuries. They'd interviewed the woman when she came out of surgery. She said she hadn't seen anything—everybody panicked, it was a mob scene.

I thought about the gun in her hand. That woman, his bodyguard, she wouldn't say anything, ever. She wasn't his woman—it was business.

♦

I waited a couple of days, then I went to see Monroe. He was sitting where he was before. All the same people with him, except for the redheaded guy.

"Ghost! Like a fucking ghost, just like I said. How'd you do it?"

"Did you find her?" I asked him.

"I got feelers out all over the place. Don't worry about it. She's out there, I'll find her for you. Where do I . . . ?"

"I'll come back," I told him.

◆

When I came back in another week, he asked me if I had a picture of Shella. I never had a picture of Shella.

◆

Two more weeks went by. I went to see Monroe. I just stood there, looking down at him.

"You scare me sometimes, Ghost," he said. "Look, I can't come up with the girl, how about I just pay you the money instead?"

"No. That's wasn't what you said."

"Okay, okay. I'm still looking, got feelers out all over the place. Remember what I told you? Maybe she's not working. . . . She's in jail or married or something, it could take a long time to track her down. It ain't like you got any ID on her."

"I know. I'll wait."

◆

I told Misty I'd be going soon. On a trip. Somebody was looking for an old friend of mine. When they found her, I'd go out there to see her.

"In Chicago? Is that where you'll be going?"

"I don't know. Wherever she is."

"Remember when we first talked about it? In the car? I always wanted to try Chicago."

I didn't say anything.

The next morning, Misty got home from the club, took her shower, got in bed with me. I was awake.

"Honey, remember when I was telling you about the ladies' room? In the club where we went dancing? I didn't mean to give you the wrong idea."

"About what?"

"What the girls were doing in there. The lesbian stuff. When I said it was disgusting . . . ? I didn't mean doing it was disgusting . . . just, in the toilet like that, in front of everyone, you know what I mean?"

"Sure."

"I mean . . . some men, they think it's the most beautiful thing. To watch. You ever notice that? Like in porno movies . . . ? Guys'll watch two women going at it, really get turned on. But you never see women watching movies of men doing each other. How come you think that is?"

"I don't know."

"You ever . . . go to one of those movies?"

I did, once. A gay movie. The guy I was paid to do, he went there all the time. Cruising, they call it. It was the easiest one I ever did. I just sat in the back where they told me. The guy came in, sat down next to me. Didn't say a word at first. I just watched the movie, didn't answer when he started talking to me. I let him unzip my fly. When he put his head down, I broke his neck.

"No," I told her, rubbing her back.

"You think maybe you'd like to . . . someday?"

"No. I got nothing against them. I knew one. From when I was inside. Real hard guy, kept to himself."

"I don't mean *men*, honey. Girls."

"I don't go to the movies much."

"I know. But you liked that time we went, didn't you?"

"Sure." It was called *Goodfellas*. A movie about gangsters. The guy who wrote it, he knew what he was doing,

how they work. It didn't seem like a movie at all, except
for the music. I wished I could have watched it without
the sound.

Misty put her hand between my legs, rolling onto her
side, talking low against my chest.

"I could bring a girlfriend home some night. From the
club, after work. Would you like that, baby?"

"Bring her here?"

"Or someplace else, if you want. There's a girl works at
the club, Chantal. She goes both ways. I know she likes
me, I can tell. We could put on a little show for you. I'd
like that, if you would. I'm not the jealous kind, I know
how to share."

"That's okay."

"You don't want me to?"

"No, it's all right."

♦

It was a Thursday night when I saw him again.

"I've been waiting for you, Ghost. Your girl's working in
Cleveland, a joint off Euclid Avenue, downtown. You know
it?"

"I've never been there," I told him. It wasn't true—I
did some work there once. Don't know why I didn't tell
Monroe.

"It's called The Chamber, this joint. Real hardcore, the
way I hear it."

He was watching my face as he was talking. He doesn't
usually do that. I put my eyes at the top of his nose, right
between his eyebrows.

He lit a cigar. "She's using the name Roxie. She's not on

the books—the manager says she only works part-time, Friday, Saturday night, like that."

"Thanks."

"Anytime, Ghost. I'm a man of my word. Besides, I wouldn't want you getting mad at me, coming back to see me."

"I wouldn't do that."

He gave me the address of the club, asked me how I would get there. I told him I'd drive out, take a couple of days.

◆

I called Cleveland information from a pay phone. They didn't have a listing for this Chamber place. It didn't mean anything. Some of the clubs, they advertise in the Yellow Pages and all, some of them just have a pay phone in the back.

◆

I told Misty I'd be gone a couple of days, maybe a little longer. Packed some stuff in an airline bag. She sat on the bed, watching me.

"You'll be back?"

"Sure."

"You promise?"

"Why you asking me all this?"

"I'm sorry. I mean . . . I know we don't . . . just . . . I thought we could . . . keep on. . . ."

"It's okay," I told her.

◆

I took a plane into Cleveland, told the cab driver to take me to an address I remembered. On the West Side, near the water. They call it The Flats, this section.

When I got out of the cab, it had all changed. Last time I was there, it was a rough neighborhood. Waterfront bars, strip joints, whores on the street, places where you could rent a room, nobody asked your name. Now it was all fancy restaurants, little shops where you could buy expensive stuff, looked all new.

I went further along the West Side, out on Detroit Avenue. Finally, I found a place, little sign said ROOMS. I paid the man some money. Everybody had hillbilly accents. The room was small, bathroom down the hall.

◆

That night I went to the club. It was right where Monroe said it would be. No pictures of the girls on the outside. Man at the door, all dressed in black.

"Members only," he told me.

I turned to walk away. I was going to wait until the place closed, talk to Shella when she came out.

"Membership costs twenty bucks," the man said.

I gave him a twenty, went inside. It was dark, like a cave. A woman was standing next to a post, hands wrapped in leather straps high above her head. A little red ball was in her mouth, a strap around the back of her head like a gag. She had no clothes on. Another woman stood next to her, high black boots that came almost to her knees, a black corset pulled tight around her waist. When I walked past, she said "Fifty bucks." I kept walking over to the bar, asked the man for a rum and Coke like I always do.

I sipped the Coke, watched. Two women came over to the girl tied to the post. They gave some money to the woman in the corset. She picked up a leather handle with thin straps attached to it, whipped the other woman three times.

People were all in costumes. Masks, chains. It smelled like a hospital where somebody was going to die.

A stairway in one corner. Doors to rooms on the side. It felt like the ceiling was very low but I couldn't see it.

I looked around some more. No stage. No dancers.

When the bartender came back, I asked him if Roxie was on tonight.

He looked at me close, for just a second. Told me she wasn't—wait there and he'd find out for me, when she was coming back.

A man sat down next to me, another man with him, a studded collar around his neck. The first man held a leash to the collar. He asked me for a match.

I gave him a little box of wooden matches. He said thanks. Struck a match, held it against the hand of the man on the leash. I could see the flesh burn, but the man on the leash didn't say anything.

The bartender came back. Said Roxie would be coming back on Tuesday. I thanked him, left ten dollars on the bar.

I walked out. When I got on the sidewalk, I turned left, looking for a cab. A man in a raincoat came out of the alley. I was on him before he could get the sawed-off out of his coat—I heard the shotgun go off as my fingers went for his eyes, felt a stinging against my legs, twisted my body against the wall, and pulled him down with me. Shots came from in front of me, chipping the brick wall. The man's body caught a couple of them, one nipped the fleshy part of my arm.

A siren ripped out. I heard shoes slapping on the sidewalk. I bent down to make sure the shotgun man was finished. The sawed-off was on a leather strap around his neck so he could swing it free when he needed it. A photograph was taped to the inside forearm of his coat. My picture, black and white. I pulled it free.

I left the man's body there, kept moving through the alley. Came out on the next block. Started walking.

◆

I walked for a long time. A black girl came up to me, asked me if I wanted to have a party. I asked her how much. She said twenty-five, ten for the room.

I told her okay, gave her the money. She took me to this hotel, signed the book for us. We went upstairs.

Little room, one light bulb hanging from the ceiling. The sheets were yellowish, washbasin in one corner. There was no chair. I sat on the bed.

"You want some half 'n' half, honey? Get your motor started?"

"Unbutton my coat," I told her.

She did it. My shirt was red around the muscle. "Take it off," I said.

She knew what I meant. Was real careful about it. There was a slash across my arm—the bullet hadn't gone in.

"Can you get some hot water here?"

"Down the hall, honey."

"Here's what I want. You get me some hot water, okay? Real hot. I'll put my arm on the windowsill, you pour the water across it. Then you tie my shirt around it. Tight. Tight as you can. Then I'm gone. I'll give you another fifty bucks, okay?"

She nodded. I gave her the fifty. Opened the window with my left hand in case she didn't come back quick.

But she did. She poured the hot water over my arm. It ran off clean, but it was bleeding a lot.

She took some stuff out of her purse. Kotex. "It ain't much, but it'll be better than just that shirt, okay?"

I told her thanks. She put the Kotex on my arm, tied the shirt tight around it, helped me on with my jacket.

"Where's the nearest city?" I asked her.

"Big city? Akron, I guess."

"Want to make a couple of hundred bucks?"

"Doing what?"

"Can you get a car?"

"No, honey. I ain't got no car. My man, he's got a car. Nice big car. You want I should . . . ?"

"No. Just give me a hand downstairs, hail a cab for me."

She did it, standing on the sidewalk in her bright-blue dress.

I got in, told the driver to take me to the bus station.

I caught the next bus out to Chicago.

♦

In Chicago, I found a room near the middle of town. The Loop, the cab driver called it.

By the next day, my arm wasn't bleeding anymore. I changed the dressing, used my undershirt.

I went out, found an army-navy store, bought a couple of sweatshirts, a pair of pants.

I got a razor and some other stuff in a drugstore.

When I was clean, I took a cab to the airport, bought a ticket to Philadelphia.

I took a bus from there to Port Authority, then I walked to the hotel.

◆

When I let myself into the room, I could feel how empty it was. Misty's clothes were gone from the closet. There was a note on the bed.

I don't know how to say this. I hope you come back and read this, and I also hope you never come back, and then you won't read this. I don't know, I'm leaving, you don't want me anyway. I need to have a man, I guess that makes me weak. Maybe you don't need anybody. I don't think you do. I know you're looking for her, whoever she is, but I don't know why. I guess it doesn't matter. There's a man who comes in the club, he asked me did I want to move in with him. I never said I would, I never even went with him, not while I was with you, but I'm going now. I paid the room rent for three weeks, so they wouldn't put your stuff out. If you're not back by then, I guess maybe you're not coming back. I never knew your name. But I did love you, I swear.

◆

I lay down on the bed, closed my eyes. Thinking, I have to go see Monroe before I start looking for Shella again.

JOHN

I'm not a plotter. Shella always said the only thing that kept me from going to jail all the time was patience. Because I always know how to wait.

I tried to think it through. Monroe, he never knew where Shella was. He could never find her—it was all talk. Liar's talk. Big, boasting talk, showing off. But it worked on me. He was my hope—I made him into something and he just played it out.

He used me. Then he got scared.

Monroe would know I got away in Cleveland. He paid them for a body and he didn't get one. He'd be afraid now. I don't like it when people are afraid—it makes them smart. He didn't know where I was, but that wouldn't matter anyway. He'd know I'd be coming for him. And all I knew was the poolroom where he'd be.

So what he'd do, I thought about it, what he'd do is be afraid. Have a lot of people around him, watching for me. I didn't know where he lived. Nothing.

If I went back to the bar where I first connected with him, he'd know. They'd send me someplace and there'd be more people waiting for me.

I have to kill him. He lied to me. He made me lose time when I could have been looking for Shella. I did work for him and he didn't pay me. I have to kill him. I tried to talk to Shella. In my head. I couldn't see her, but I knew what she'd say.

It didn't take me long to pack. In the top drawer of the dresser, where I kept my underwear and socks, there was a picture of Misty. A big picture, black and white. In her dancer's costume, smiling. On the back was a red kiss, in lipstick. Tiny little writing under it, in pencil. "In case you ever want to look for me, I'll be there." And a phone number. The area code was 904. There was a phone book in the room. In the front, it had a map of the country, with little spaces marked off. What the area code covered. 904 was the top part of Florida.

♣

Nobody paid any attention to me when I walked through the lobby—the room rent was paid. I got my car out of the garage, paid the man, and drove through the tunnel to Jersey.

♣

I followed the turnpike. Right at the speed limit. All the way through Pennsylvania into Ohio. I pulled over in Youngstown, got a motel room, slept a long time.

The next night, I drove past Cleveland, right on through to Indiana. Got off near Gary, found another room.

I slept through the day again.

That night, I found the strip, just outside of town. They all look the same, those bars. There's so many.

No sign of Shella.

♣

In the morning, I kept going west. When I saw the signs for Chicago, I pulled over by a pay phone. I dialed the number Misty had left. A woman's voice answered. Young woman.

"Could I speak to Misty?" I asked the voice.

"She's not here right now. If you'll leave me a number, I'll have her call you back."

I hung up. I guess the woman was Misty's friend. Maybe Misty would call her once in a while, check in. Everybody has a friend.

♣

Stony Island Avenue, that's what the sign said. The whole neighborhood was black, but a lot of people in the cars were white. A pass-through zone. I got back in the car, pulled in behind a white man in one of the those rich, dark boxy foreign sedans. I just followed him until we got downtown, then I peeled off and drove around until I found a place where I could park.

I bought a couple of newspapers. Then I found a room and went to sleep.

♣

At night, I went to some of the places I found in the newspapers. The more you pay, the nearer the girls get. Like bait. Table dancers, lap dancers. Some of the girls could dance, most of them couldn't. Some of them could act—it looked like they were really getting worked up doing what they did. Most of them, they just looked glazed. Nobody looked at anyone's face.

I kept spending money. Not that much money—I didn't have to get that close to know if it was Shella.

One joint had a sign in front: LIVE GIRLS. It made me think about something, but it didn't stay in my mind. I went inside. It was the same.

♣

The next night, I went north. Uptown, they called it. The first place I tried said TOPLESS, but it was full of hard drinkers, not even looking at the girls.

In another joint, I was sitting at a table near the back. A big guy in a shirt cut off to show his muscles was sitting at the next table, yelling at the girls, calling them fucking dykes, cunts, all like that. The bouncer came over, told him he had to leave. The guy kicked up a fuss and the bouncer got his arm up behind the guy's back, walked him out the door. I didn't pay attention, just watched the front so I could see the whole selection of girls before I moved on to the next place.

I felt a hand on the back of my neck. "You too, asshole." It was the bouncer, pulling me up and out of the chair. I stood up and I felt the kidney punch coming—I got my elbow into his lower ribs as I brought my heel down hard across his ankle. His hand let go—his face came over my right shoulder and I kept it going into the top of the table.

People were watching. I got up. The bouncer fell on the floor. In the front, the girls were still moving their bodies, the music was still loud.

I went out the front door. The guy in the cut-off shirt

was walking up the street toward the bar. There was a gun in his hand. His face was crazy.

♣

I didn't go far. Whatever I did in the bar, the guy with the muscles was about to do worse. The cops would be coming. I found another bar in the next block, not a strip joint. They were playing music up on a little stage in front, chicken wire all across, like they were in a cage. I tried to sit in the back, listen to the music. Country music, I guess it was. It was so loud my head hurt. One guy finished his bottle of beer and threw it at the musicians. I saw what the chicken wire was for—they kept right on playing.

After about an hour, I left. It was still early.

The last bar I went to, it was like a place where people do business. The waitresses were topless, and they had dancers and all, but they had booths in the back. I saw men talking to each other, not even watching the girls.

One booth was empty. I ordered a steak sandwich and a rum and Coke from the girl, did what I always do.

I was just going to leave when the Indian sat down across from me.

♣

He put his hands on the table, turned them over once, like it was a secret greeting I'd recognize. All I could tell was his hands were empty. I looked to my left, kept one hand under the table, measuring the distance to him in my mind.

"There's nobody else," he said, like he knew what I was thinking.

I just watched him, listening to the sounds of the joint,

feeling for a change in the rhythm. If there was anyone else, I couldn't pick them up.

Time passed. He nodded over at the pack of cigarettes I had on the tabletop. "Okay?" he asked.

I nodded back. He shook one out, lit it with the paper matches I had there.

He smoked the whole cigarette through, real calm, smoking like he was enjoying it, not nervous or anything. His right hand had a long jagged scar across the back. He ground out the smoke in the ashtray.

"You all right with this now?" he said.

"All right with what?"

"This place. Talking to me."

"Talk about what?" Thinking that maybe he had others outside—by now he'd had enough time to surround the place.

"I followed you from Morton's."

"Morton's?"

"Where you dumped that bouncer."

"I don't know what you're talking about."

"I know. I want to talk to you . . . about some work."

"I'm not looking for work."

"Not a factory, my friend. Not a car wash either. Your work. It's my work too."

"What?"

"I know what you do. I have work for you. You want it or not?"

"No."

He just sat there, the way people sit in prison. Like time doesn't matter, even the time they're doing. I was going to leave first, give him my back. The waitress came over. He didn't stare at her breasts, just ordered a hamburger and a Coke.

"Costs the same as liquor," the waitress told him.

"That's all right. And bring my friend another of whatever he's drinking over there."

The waitress took away my empty shot glass and the water glass with the Coke and melted ice in the bottom. I ate in a place once where they emptied the ashtray with you sitting right at the table—emptied it into a napkin, left a fresh one there for you. She didn't do that. In joints like the one we were in, they take away the empty drink glasses so you don't sit there sucking on the ice. And so you don't keep track of how many you had.

She brought the guy his hamburger, set up my drinks. I sipped the Coke. He nodded, like I was telling him something.

"You really an Indian?" I asked him.

"Half Chickasaw, half Apache. My name's Wolf."

"Wolf." I said it again to myself. It didn't sound right.

He saw what I was thinking. "It's really a longer name. It means something like Wolf of Long Eyes. The spotter-wolf for the pack. But it doesn't translate so good, so I go by Wolf."

"Why'd you come after me?"

"You want to know why you didn't pick me up, tracking you?" I didn't know how he could tell that. "I didn't come after you myself," he said. "I sent it out on the drums. Saw you in Morton's, got the word to my people. I just waited where I was until they got back to me. Then I came in."

"So you got a whole . . . crew out there?"

"Uptown's got the largest collection of off-reservation Indians in America. Different tribes, but it don't matter to the whites. They can't see us, can't tell us apart—it's like having yellow skin in the Orient."

"You been in the Orient?"

"Oh yes. Vietnam. Where I learned my trade. Where'd you learn?"

I didn't say anything, wondering how he knew.

"You don't use guns, do you?" he asked, like we were talking about fishing tackle or something. "We all use different things, get the work done. Is that a special style?"

"Style?"

"Like kung fu, or akido, you know what I mean. I never saw anyone do that before . . . put all their weight in one place."

"What do you want?" I asked him again. Thinking maybe this was the end of it for me. You hear about other guys in the business, how some of them like to make a ceremony out of it, talk to the target before they get it done. Telling me about his tribe and all . . . maybe he was trying to tell me I could take him out but it wouldn't help, there'd be others outside.

"I heard about you," he said. "Not your name. I heard about you for years."

"Not me."

"Oh yeah. You. I earned my name. I'm never wrong. I saw death through a little round circle of glass so many times, until it got so I could see it through concrete. You and me, we're the same. Brothers in the blood. There's men who hunt for trophies, go out into the woods in a Jeep wearing pretty clothes and blast a deer through a scope. They stalk, but they don't see. You and me, we hunt for meat. Meat to eat, meat to live. It's how we live. It's how the pack hunts."

"I don't have a pack."

"I know. But you don't do it for fun."

"Fun?"

"They call themselves professionals. You know, the greaseballs in the fancy suits, dogs on leashes, do what they're told. They don't have a pack either, they just think they do. And when the bracelets come on, they start to sing. Rats run in packs too, but they don't live for the pack, they live for themselves. There's psychos too. They like the taste. After a while, they get to need it. You're one of us, you just don't know it."

"I'm not anything."

The waitress came back, cleared off the Indian's dishes. He held up his empty glass, looked over at me.

"I'm okay," I said.

♣

The girls were circulating around the tables, getting the men to buy them watered drinks. They didn't come near the booths.

"You're looking for a woman," the Indian said. Like it wasn't a question.

"I'm not looking for anybody."

"You're not hunting," the Indian said. "You were hunting, you'd be looking for a man. It wouldn't take you that long to see if he was in a place. You go in and out, watch the dancers, make sure you see the whole shift. Then you try another place. It's a woman you're looking for."

I thought about it. I'd never find Shella the way I was going. After Monroe . . .

"If I was . . . ?"

"Nobody knows Uptown like my people do," the Indian said. "If she's here, I'll find her for you."

"For what?"

"What? For what? What's that mean?"

"What do you want? In exchange."

"Does it matter?" he asked me.

♣

I told him about Shella. I can see her better when I talk about her . . . that's why I do it in my head. He listened, that's all he did, waiting for me to finish.

"There's things you can make different," he said when I was done. "Lose weight, gain weight. Contact lenses. Cut your hair, dye it a new color. You can cover scars, change tattoos. Buy a whole new face, you got the money."

"I know."

"And things you can't." Like I hadn't said anything. "You don't have a picture, right?"

"No."

"Show me how tall she is, barefoot."

I held my hand just between my eyebrows and my hairline, like a salute.

He turned over the menu, just a blank piece of white paper on the back. "Show me the distance between the centers of her eyes."

I put my hand on the paper, spread my thumb and forefinger, closed my eyes, seeing her face. When I got it right, I opened my eyes. He took a black grease pencil out of his pocket, put a little dot at each end of the space I made. I took my hand away. He connected the dots, as straight and true as a ruler. Folded the paper, put it in his pocket.

"She ever get busted?"

"Yes."

"More than once?"

"Yes."

"Felony pops?"

I nodded.

"Ever do time?"

"Not real time. Not since she's been grown. Ten days here, a week there. Sweep arrests, a stolen car once. Nothing big."

"Maybe they'd have printed her?"

"Sure."

"We can't look past Uptown," the Indian said. "Don't come back here."

♣

I tried other places around Chicago. Music bars on Rush Street, fancy joints near the lake, dives on the South Side.

When I got back early one morning, the Indian was waiting in my room.

♣

I didn't ask him how he got in—I'm no good at it, but I know it's easy to do.

"She's not in Uptown," the Indian said.

"Thanks anyway," I told him, but he didn't get up to go like I expected.

"If she was printed, I know someone who could find her."

"Who?"

"A crazy man. He's a trader. Never pays money for work. We did something for him . . ."

I just looked at him, waiting.

". . . and he made good. Did what he said."

"Somebody told me that once . . . that they could find her."

"It'd work the same way as a job—he'd have to pay up front."

"You work for him?"

"No."

"What's in it for you?"

"There's something we have to do. Not you and me, we . . . my people and me, okay? There's places we can't go. Where you could just walk in."

"And I do this work, this work for you, and then I get to see this guy, right?"

His face was sad, like I told him somebody just died. "No," is all he said.

I waited in that room. He lit a cigarette, smoked it all the way through. I didn't move.

He ground out his cigarette butt on the windowsill, took a deep breath.

"I'll take you to him. He'll ask you some questions, make sure you're the right man. If he makes the deal, he'll find her for you. Wherever she is. Then you do it. Whatever he wants. When you finish with him, you do this thing for us. Then it's done."

"And he'll find Shella for me?"

"He'll find her. No promises what he'll find. She could be in jail, could be dead." He looked over at me. "She could be with a man," he said, like that was worse.

"I know."

"And you get it up front. But if he finds her, you owe him. Straight up."

"And you too."

"Me too."

I told him I'd do it.

♣

I didn't look around Chicago anymore. Just waited on the Indian. Stayed in my room. There was no TV, so I listened to the radio. It was mostly hillbilly music. I kept it turned down low, next to my head. They played this song once, I never heard the name of it. A man's going to be hanged in the morning, so his woman goes to the warden. She gives him her body so he'll call the hanging off. But it happens anyway. She did it for nothing. I thought of Shella—how she'd do that.

It made me sad, being cheated that way.

♣

One morning, there was a soft tap on my door. I opened it. It was one of the gay guys who lived together at the end of the hall. His partner was standing just behind him, suitcases on the floor. I didn't say anything.

The guy who knocked was wearing an orange tank top, a fat, soft-looking man, mostly bald.

"We're moving out," he said. "Just wanted to say goodbye."

"Goodbye," I told him, watching. They never spoke to me before.

"You should go too," the man said.

I didn't say anything.

"Show him," his partner said. "Hurry up." His partner was small, dark-haired. He was wearing a white silk shirt, like a woman's blouse. He had makeup on his face, eyeliner.

"You never hassled us," the fat man said. He took some slivers of steel out of a leather case, walked next door. He

played with the lock for a second and the door came open.
I looked over his shoulder.

The room smelled ugly. Fast-food cartons all over the
place, on the floor, everywhere. In one corner there was
a high stack of magazines, up to a man's waist. On the wall,
there were pictures. A woman on her knees, ropes around
her hands behind her back, ropes around her ankles. She
was wearing a blindfold. All the pictures were like that.
Most of them were slashed, like with a razor. One woman's
face had a black X across it. The windows were sealed shut
with duct tape. Everything smelled like rot.

"The cops'll be here soon," the fat man said. "Don't open
the closet."

I turned around to leave. The little guy with the eyeliner
on his face was standing in the door, facing out. He had a
pistol in his hand, held close by his leg.

♣

I walked down the stairs to check out, my duffel bag over
my shoulder. The clerk didn't say anything, didn't even
look up.

When I hit the street, I saw an Indian working under
the hood of an old car. I moved slow, so he could see me.

I found another hotel a few blocks away. The window
looked out into an alley. The same Indian was out there,
working on the same car.

♣

About a week went by. I went for a walk one day, had
something to eat. When I opened the door to my room,
the Indian was sitting there.

"It's time," he said. "Time to meet the man."

"Okay."

"Not now. Sunday. We have to go to his office. When there's nobody around to watch. Be downstairs, five in the morning. I'll pick you up."

♣

I was there, waiting like he said. It was a cab that pulled up. The Indian was in the back seat. He didn't say anything to the driver. The cab took off. Still dark out.

I couldn't see the driver's face through the partition—he was wearing one of those chauffeur's caps. His hair was long, black.

The cab was quiet inside, moving steady, stopping for all the lights. I saw the meter in the front—it was running, like we were a fare.

We got on the highway, headed downtown.

"You're not asking any questions?" the Indian said.

"I don't have any questions," I told him.

♣

The cab pulled over. The Indian took a little black box from his pocket, pushed a button. I heard a beep from the front seat. The driver held the palm of his hand flat against the plastic partition. The Indian held his hand against it, like the way you shake hands in prison when they don't let you touch.

The Indian got out. I followed him. He had a red rose in his right hand. The building was the tallest one I ever saw—I couldn't see the top from the ground.

♣

The security guard was sitting in front of a whole bunch of little TV sets. Each one had a different picture, black and white. One looked like an underground garage.

The Indian held up the red rose. The security guard hit a switch. One of the little TV screens went blank.

We walked over to the elevators. When the door closed, the Indian pushed 88.

When we stepped off the elevator, the floor was empty.

I followed the Indian down a long corridor, all windows to our left. The doors on the right were all open, nobody inside the rooms. Clicking, beeping sounds, like machines talking to each other. The Indian moved quiet, but he moved fast. The corridor made a right-angle turn at the end, and then we started down another hallway. This was down the middle of the building, no more windows.

The Indian held up his hand. I stopped behind him. He pointed to the carpet in front of us. I looked close. There was a thin line across the hall, side to side. Another one a few feet away. I stared at it until it came clear . . . a bunch of little X's covering about four feet, longer than any man's stride. The Indian held his finger to his lips, pointed to the spot on the carpet where the X's started. He stepped back, took a short run, and jumped over that section. He walked off a few feet to give me room—then I did the same thing he did.

We made one more turn and the Indian walked into an office. A man was at a desk, typing something. He was facing away from us, next to a big window. The Indian tapped on the door frame. The man spun around, like he was surprised to see us.

The Indian walked in, took a seat in front of the desk. I sat down next to him. On the man's computer screen I saw what looked like the floor plan of a building.

The man turned to face us. He had a long neck, a small head. Like a weasel. There was a big lump over one eye, bulging. The lump was pale, even whiter than his face. His eyes were bright blue, like the neon signs they use to get you inside the strip joints.

"You don't make much noise, Chief," the man said.

The Indian didn't say anything.

"Is this him?" the man asked.

The Indian nodded.

The man looked at me like he expected someone else. He turned away from us, tapped keys on his computer. Stuff came up on the screen, black on a white background. Too far away for me to read.

"You ever been in Houston?" he asked me.

I didn't answer him.

"Ever been in the Four Seasons Hotel on Lamar? In Houston?"

I watched him. The Indian didn't move.

"Ramon del Vega was found in a room there. With his neck broken. Looked like a robbery. Except he had a gold-and-diamond Rolex still on his wrist. Almost nine thousand cash in his pockets."

I didn't say anything. I remembered the guy. The people who set it up, they had me registered in that hotel. I got a call. The voice just said "Now" and hung up. I went to the top floor, taking the stairs. Saw the room-service waiter outside the door with a tray. I stood there against the wall. As the waiter was bowing his way out, his hand full of cash, I stepped inside through the open door. The guy inside started to say something. I broke his neck. Then I went back to my room. Two men came to my room, gave me the money I was promised. I checked out before they found the body.

I never knew the guy's name before this.

The man with the lump on his head kept tapping the keys, asking me more questions. I sat there, listening. The man rubbed the lump on his head.

"You're sure this is him?" he asked the Indian again.

The Indian got up, walked over to the side of the room. There was a postage meter, one of those electronic scales. The Indian made a gesture for me to come over, stand by him. The man got up from his desk, came over with us. He walked twisted. Standing next to me, he was much shorter. One leg was in a big crooked boot that laced up the front, like the foot was too big for a shoe. The Indian took something out of his pocket. Flicked his wrist, a long blade shot out. He put the knife on the postal scale. The dial on its face lit up. It said:

0   4.3   1.21.

Then he put his hand on the scale, just barely touching it with his fingertips. The numbers flashed, kept changing. Only the first 0 stayed the same. The middle numbers jumped: 1.1, 0.9, 1.3, 0.7. The end numbers jumped too, only not as much: 0.29, 0.52.

"It reads in tenths of an ounce," the Indian said to the man. "You can't hold your hand steady enough to stop the numbers jumping. It's too sensitive."

"So?" the man said.

"Try it," the Indian told him.

The man put his hand on the scale. I could see him lock up his face, concentrating. He couldn't stop the numbers from jumping. He pushed down hard—it didn't make any difference.

"Pick a number," the Indian told the man.

The man looked at the Indian. Rubbed the lump on his head again. "Zero point six," he said.

The Indian nodded at me. I put my fingers on the scale, getting the feel, letting my fingertips go right inside my head, no wrist or arm between them. I thought about the numbers the man wanted until they came up on the face of the scale. It fluttered a little bit, then it locked in. I held it there.

"Pick another," the Indian said.

"One point eight," the man said.

I let my fingertips go heavier until the number he wanted came up. I locked it in again.

The Indian lit a cigarette. I held the numbers while he smoked it through. The man watched the scale. Then he limped over to his desk and sat down.

♣

We were sitting back across from him. Time passed. I didn't keep track of it. The man looked over at the Indian.

"So what's that prove?"

"You know what it proves," the Indian told him. "You want him to bend a crowbar in his bare hands, break some boards, crap like that?"

"I have to be sure."

"You know how to do that. What you told me. About Raiford."

"He'll sit for it?" The crazy man talked. Talking like I wasn't there.

"You got Wants and Warrants?" the Indian asked.

"No."

"You told me he jumped parole."

The man rubbed his lump again. "You trust me? I could get him pulled in, he's the same guy."

"You won't."

The man sat there for a few minutes. Then he got up, limped over to something that looked like a Xerox machine. He lifted up the cover, turned it on. It made a whining noise. Then he went back to the computer, tapped some more keys. "Okay," he said to the Indian, "let's run him."

The Indian got up, gestured to me to follow. He spread his hand out, palm down, pointed to the glass plate on the Xerox machine. I put my whole palm against it. Left it there for a minute.

"Okay," the man said from his desk.

The Indian took a spray can from next to the Xerox, wiped off the glass.

We sat down again. Waited.

In a few minutes, there was a beep from the computer screen. The man hit the keys again, read the screen.

"It's you," he said.

♣

The Indian and I smoked a couple of cigarettes apiece while the man played with his computer. He spun around in his chair to face us.

"The PVW is off," he said.

"Parole Violation Warrant," the Indian said. Looking at the man, explaining it to me.

"Yes. You're dead," he said to me. "Killed in a train wreck in South Carolina. Amtrak out of D.C., heading for Florida. Unidentified white man, mangled pretty bad. We just ran his prints, got a match with yours. You're off the computers. Dead."

I didn't say anything.

"You know what I want?" the man asked, looking right into my eyes.

I nodded.

"I find your girl, you do this for me . . . that's our deal?"

I nodded again.

"Show us," the Indian said.

"What?"

"You know *he* can do it. . . . Show us *you* can."

The man smiled. His teeth were yellow, crooked, all mashed together in his mouth. He went back to his computer.

♣

"Huntsville, Alabama," the man said.

I watched him.

"Room 907. Marilyn Hammond. Executive VP for an options-trading firm on the coast. Declared an income of one hundred and eighty-eight thousand dollars last year. She's a white female, five foot four, a hundred and fifty-one pounds. Brown hair, brown eyes. Divorced, no kids. That's what she's doing now."

"That's not Shella," I told him.

"No, that's not her, that's what she *does*. This Marilyn, she's heavy into S&M. That's the way she gets off. Your Shella, she's a hardcore top, you understand? After you went down in Florida, she took off. But she didn't go back to dancing . . . she disappeared into the fem-dom underground."

"Disappeared?"

"She can't hide," the man said. "It's easy to find fetish

players. All they think about is their games. It's perfect for your girl . . . she doesn't even have to be an outlaw. She's not even selling sex now. They advertise in the magazines. Role-playing. Discipline sessions. All that stuff. I can find her."

I thought about that cottage we'd rented a long time ago. That girl, Bonnie. Shella slapping her.

♣

"We have a deal?" the man asked me.

"We're changing the deal," the Indian said.

The man rubbed the lump on his head, not saying anything.

"We want to do your work first," the Indian said. "Then, when you find his woman, he doesn't have to come back and see you."

The man smiled his smile again. "So what I promised you for bringing him to me, for getting him to do the work . . . you don't want to wait for that either?"

"No," the Indian said.

"You're worried he's going to find his girl and take off . . . not come back and do the work?"

"No."

"What if he does the work and I don't find the girl for him?"

"You will."

"You threatening me?"

"Yes."

The man turned to me. "You okay with this? You do the work for me first, then I find the girl?"

"You look while I'm working," I told him.

"The Chief here will tell you what I need done, okay?"

"Yes."

"When it's done, you get your girl."

I nodded.

"I can find her," the man said. "I can find anyone."

I just looked at him—this part was over.

"I found you," the man said.

♣

As we stepped outside, a cab pulled up. A different one. We got in the back. The Indian didn't say anything to the driver.

When we turned into the block near where I was staying, the Indian turned to me.

"Get your stuff, check out, okay?"

I did what he told me. The cab was still waiting out front. I put my duffel bag in the trunk.

"You got a car around here?" he asked me.

"Yes."

"Give me the keys." I did it. "Show me where it is." The cab pulled up next to my car.

"I'll follow in your car, okay?" the Indian said.

♣

The cab went along Broadway, turned into a block lined with apartment buildings on both sides. The sign said Carmen Avenue. The cab came to a stop. The driver didn't say anything.

I smoked a cigarette. After a while, the Indian opened the back door. I got out. We took my duffel bag from the trunk. I followed the Indian inside the building. It was a big apartment, long. It went all the way through: windows on the street, windows out back, into an alley. My car was parked back there.

The Indian opened the refrigerator, showed me there was food inside. Furniture in the apartment, like somebody lived there. He gave me two keys. "One's the front door downstairs, one's for this place. The rent's paid, nobody'll bother you. There's a phone in the living room. When you hear it ring, pick it up, don't say anything. If it's me, I'll talk. If you don't hear my voice, just hang up." He gave me back my car keys too.

"I'll be back tomorrow morning," the Indian said. "I'll call first. Anybody rings the bell downstairs, don't pay attention."

"I got it."

He turned like he was going to go. Then he spun around and faced me. Stuck out his hand, open. I didn't know.
. . . I put out my own hand. He grabbed it, squeezed, hard. I squeezed back, careful not to hurt him.

Then he went out the door.

♣

I opened my duffel bag, laid out my stuff. Took a shower. Turned on the TV set. I left the sound off, watching the pictures in the front room. The curtains were closed—it was like night.

A nature show came on. A snake caught a big fat furry animal. It swallowed the furry animal, a big bulge all through its body.

The snake was a monster. Dangerous to anybody. But

when it was all stuffed with food, it could hardly move. And it couldn't bite.

♣

I made a sandwich, took some cold water from the refrigerator. When I finished, I smoked a cigarette. The telephone was one of those old black ones, with a dial instead of push buttons. I looked at it for a while.

I don't know one single phone number. Not one.

I tried to think about what happened. It's hard for me. I asked Shella if I was stupid, once. A long time ago. Her face got sad.

"You're not stupid, baby. Not like dumb-stupid. You don't get things because you don't feel them, that's all. Like your brain is all scar tissue."

"I never got hit in the head. Not real hard, anyway."

"You just do it different than most people. There's things we don't want to remember. I worked with a girl once. She was a real racehorse, a sleek girl with legs that went on forever. Everybody called her Rose . . . 'cause she had such long stems, get it?"

"I guess. . . ."

"Oh, shut up. Just listen for a minute. Rose was hooking big-time. Worked out-call, never less than five yards a night. She didn't draw lines, a three-way girl, she'd take it anyplace you wanted to put it. You get *that*, right?"

"Yes."

"She killed a trick. Stabbed him to death with a letter opener. The papers said he didn't have a drop of blood left in him when she was done. She didn't even try and run for it—the cops found her right there. I went to visit her in the jailhouse. At first, it was like she didn't recognize me. I held her hand. Then her eyes snapped and she knew who I was. I asked her what happened. She just said . . . 'Flashback.' That's all she said. Flashback.

"At her trial, the doctor said something happened to her when she was a kid. He didn't know what it was. Rose wouldn't tell him. Rose looked like a million bucks at the trial, flashing those long legs, smiling. The doctor said it was more important to her not to go back where she was —it would cost her too much.

"They found her guilty. Got a life sentence. I kissed her goodbye. She was still smiling.

"It wasn't even a year later that I read about it in the papers. She escaped. With a guard that was working her section of the prison. He was married, had two kids. They never found either of them."

"What do you think happened?" I asked her.

"I don't know. Something ugly."

"No, I mean . . ."

"Oh. I figure Rose got the guard's nose open. Some men, they'll give up everything for a taste."

"You think I'm like that?"

"You? No, honey. I don't think you're like anything. Whatever you buried, you put it down deep."

♣

I tried to think about it. The chocolate bar, when I was a kid. How it felt when I broke Duke's face open with that sock full of batteries. Swinging that sock, I knew if I didn't finish him I'd be gone. There'd be nothing left of me, I'd just disappear. Like every part of my body was in my arm

. . . it felt like a feather when I moved it, but it weighed a ton when it came down. Little explosions in my head, like light bulbs breaking. Pop. Pop. Pop. A thousand of them.

They still go off in my head when I work. But only a couple of them now.

I tried to think about what Shella said that time. But all I could think about was that she went to Rose's trial. Said goodbye to her before she went down.

♣

The phone rang in the morning. I picked it up, didn't say anything.

"I'm on my way up." The Indian's voice.

The front door to the apartment opened. The Indian stepped in, a key in his hand. We sat down in the front room.

"What do you want to know?" he asked me.

"Just where it is."

"The work?"

"Yes."

"It's not that simple. *You're* not that simple. You think that crazy little man in that high office can't make somebody dead if he wants them gone? He's a rogue. Some kind of genius, I guess. I don't know the name of the agency he plays for. Every time I have to meet him, he's in a different place. Always with his machines, like a guy with bad kidneys—he has to be hooked up every day or he dies. One of our brothers is in the basement at Marion. You know what that is?"

I nodded to tell him I did. Marion's the max-max federal

joint, the hardest one they have. And the basement is for the men who are monsters even in there.

"He can fix it. Get our brother out of there. He can't spring him free, not put him on the street. But he can get him transferred to another place. Where we can work something out later."

"What did he do, your brother?"

"What he did was, he took the weight. They got him down as a big-time serial killer. Ten, twelve bodies, all over the country. They dropped him for one. Cold and clean, no way around it. It was a setup. He came out of the room holding an empty shotgun. They let him do the work, then they took him. The crazy man sent for him—he had his machines hooked up right inside the jail where they were holding him. He told our brother he knew about the tribe, made him an offer. Our brother, he pleaded guilty to all the hits we did going back a few years. The cops cleared the books, the heat's off us. And our brother's down for forever."

"And he springs him for what?"

"For finding you, which we did. For bringing you to him. Which we did. And for you doing that piece of work."

"He'll do it?"

"Sure. He knows about our tribe. He knows me. But he doesn't know all of us. He goes back on it, any of it, we'll take him out. Whatever it costs. He knows that much about us, about our honor."

He saw me looking at him. Shook his head, lit a cigarette.

"That's our legend, that's who we are. When we say we'll do something, that's what you get. Or we die. Any one of us gives his word, he has to do it or die. And if he dies, the word goes to the next one. If we all die, the legend

still lives. We're not cheats, or liars. We're not thieves.
We're assassins."

"I . . ."

"Assassins, my friend. Hunters, feeding our families.
Only we hunt humans, not animals. We were driven off
our land. Some of us imitated the conquerors. Some of us
turned to liquor. But the warriors among us, they have
always stood in the mountains, watching the white man's
fires. We are their children. You can hire us, but you can't
own us."

"How many men . . . ?"

He waved his hand, like a mosquito was near his face.
"Men? It's all of us. Our women are more dangerous than
we are. They do our work too. And we raise our children
to follow."

"Kids?"

"The white man raises his children to rule. We raise ours
to hunt."

"Why don't you just do it yourselves? What the man
wants?"

"We can't get close enough to the target. And we never
could."

I lit a smoke of my own. He wasn't saying anything now,
waiting on me.

"Your brother, the one who's in prison?"

"Yes?"

"You send him letters and stuff? Go to see him on visiting
day?"

He nodded his head. Slow, the way you talk to a dope.
So he'll understand. "Sure," he said.

♣

He took a picture out of his bag. A black-and-white photograph. A man, maybe fifty years old. He had a round, fat face, short blond hair. More pictures. A mug shot, front and side. The man was smiling in the mug shot—I never saw that before. Close-up pictures of his arms. Tattoo of an eagle. The eagle was holding a black man in his claws. On the other arm was a hangman's noose. The words Aryan Justice were underneath it. Another picture: the man was standing in front of a crowd, waving his arms. Some of the crowd had shaved heads, some had real long hair, mustaches. They all had weapons: rifles, pistols. The Indian turned the picture over. On the back: 7/5/39, 6'1", 235, blond/blue.

"That's him," the Indian said.

♣

"It don't seem so hard to me," I told the Indian. "This guy, he speaks in front of crowds and all."

"He doesn't go on the street. Doesn't go out at all. He lives inside a compound . . . like a fort, understand? The only way to get inside, you have to be one of them."

"So why can't you . . . ?"

"You have to be white to be one of them."

"Don't they have . . . ? I mean, the crazy man, he has guys work for him."

"Undercovers? Forget it. They could never get inside. This guy, he's the boss of a crew. And they've got an acid test. You know what that is?"

"No."

"Like an initiation. Something you got to do before you even get to meet the man."

"What's the test?"

"You got to kill a black man. See? That's why they can't go inside. He's got too many buffers, too many layers. By the time you get inside, you're already outside, see? Outside the world."

"How do you know all this?"

"The crazy man explained it to me. See, sometimes, one of the followers, he turns. Rolls over. He gets dropped for something, he makes a deal. So we know how they work. Anyway, the crazy man tried it. Tried to put someone inside. Set up a phony hit on paper, made this black guy disappear, like the undercover killed him. Turned out that wasn't the test . . . you got to do a kill right in front of them. So they can see it. This guy, he thought he was inside, but he was in the ground."

"They killed him?"

"That's what the crazy man says. Says he can't prove it either. They never even found the body. Now the head man, he's more careful than he ever was. They'll never make a case against him."

"So the crazy man, he wants . . ."

"Revenge. He lost a man, he has to make it right. It's not like for us, not like loyalty. It's like . . . I can't explain it, it's like someone fucked with his machines or something. He was telling me about it, he kept saying he just needed a better plan, that's all. Just a better plan."

"And that's me?"

"That's all of us. You're just the end-piece."

"He could find my Shella?"

"Dead or alive, my friend. Guaranteed."

"If she was . . . dead, how would I know it was really her that died? He just made *me* dead, on paper, right? Couldn't he do it for her?"

"Yeah. We thought of that. So we told him, she turns up dead, he'll have to prove it. She's been busted, they probably have her prints. Or a picture. Something. He said, you wanted it, he could find some of her relatives, prove it to you that way. Okay?"

"Yes."

"You know any of her relatives? You'd know them if you meet them?"

"Yeah. I'll do it. But if Shella turns up dead, tell him I want to meet her father. I'll know him."

"It's a deal," the Indian said.

♣

I'm not like Shella. Sometimes, when we had to stay in a room for a few days, she would get all jumpy. Make up excuses why she needed to go out. Try on different outfits, do her hair different ways, take a dozen showers. There was nothing she wanted to watch on television—once she smacked the set so hard she broke it.

If I didn't have to work, maybe I'd never go out.

The Indian told me he'd need some time to scope things out, find the best way to get me inside, close to the man I had to fix.

I waited for the Indian to come back.

♣

He came one morning, told me we were going to take a ride. It was a big car. I sat in the back seat with the Indian. There were two more of them in the front.

We drove for a while. The signs kept saying North. Different routes. The Indians didn't say much. Even when they did, I couldn't understand most of it. They were speaking English and all, but the words were funny.

The roads got smaller and smaller. Concrete to blacktop to dirt. We turned onto a little path. The car had to go slow. There was a big house and a barn. A couple of dogs ran out to meet the car. They didn't bark or anything, just watched.

We drove into the barn. Everybody got out. The two in the front seat went off.

"There's a bathroom over there," the Indian pointed for me. I didn't have to use it, but I figured this was something he was telling me, so I went in. When I came out, a few of them were standing around.

They all had guns.

I wondered if Monroe knew any Indians.

♣

We walked back in the woods. There was a pond. Quiet.

"It's our land," the Indian said. "We own it. We bought it. Paid for it. Nobody comes on our land. Not now."

We kept walking. Something moved in the woods next to us. One of the dogs.

We came to a clearing. The Indian walked away from

the others. They kind of squatted on the ground, watching everything except us.

"You ever shoot a gun?" the Indian asked me.

"No."

"I didn't think so. We have to work this out, be real careful. We only get this one chance. Understand?"

"Yes." I didn't, but I knew he'd say more.

"Remember the acid test I told you about? You have to do someone. Like, just to be doing it. That should get you close enough. But you can't do it your way. If they know you work with your hands, they won't let you get close to the head man. Searching you wouldn't do any good, see? So the first job, you got to do it like a shooter. That's what we're going to show you."

"I never . . ."

"I know. You don't have to be any marksman, just know how it works."

He took a gun out of his coat. A silver gun. He squatted down. I got down next to him. He turned the gun sideways so I could see what he was doing. He pushed a piece of metal with his thumb and the round part fell sideways out of the gun. He tilted the gun in his hand and the bullets spilled out.

"There's two ways to fire this, okay? Single-action and double-action, it's called. You can cock it first, like this. . . ." He pulled back the hammer. I heard a click. "Then just pull the trigger." The gun clicked again. He slid something forward with his thumb, opened it up, held it sideways. "See? The hammer has this little spur on it. The spur comes forward, it hits the cartridge right in the center. . . ." He showed me a bullet. It had a little round dot on the back, right in the center. "That's the primer. It kicks off the powder inside, and the bullet shoots out the front. You see?"

"Yes."

"Or you can just pull the trigger without cocking it." He did it. Click, click, click. The round part turned every time he pulled the trigger.

"See how it works?"

"Yes."

He opened the gun again, handed it to me. "Look down the barrel," he said.

I did it. He made a grunting noise, took the gun out of my hand. "No. Not like that. Here, watch me." He let the light come over his shoulder, held his thumbnail where the bullet would come out, looked down the barrel from the back end. He handed it to me. I did what he did.

"What do you see?"

"It's all cut up inside. Twisted cuts."

"Those are lands and grooves. When the bullet comes through, they make it spin." He twirled his finger in the air, like a corkscrew. "It makes the bullet go straight."

"Okay."

"Hold it in your hand. Get the feel."

I took the gun. It had a heavy, solid weight. Like it was all one piece, not a bunch of parts. The grip was black rubber. I closed my eyes, getting the sense. Like a pool cue. Swinging it in little circles. I ran my fingers all over it.

I felt the Indian tap me on the shoulder.

"You go away someplace?"

"What?"

"You've been holding that piece for half a damn hour, man."

"Oh. Yeah, I guess . . ."

"You ready to learn now? Learn how to kill somebody with that thing?"

"I already know how," I told him.

He gave me a funny look. Took the gun from me, opened it up, put the bullets in. Stood there with it in his hand.

"With a pistol, you don't really aim it. You point it, just like your finger. Like it's growing out of your hand. Get a balance. . . ." He spread his legs, crouched a little bit, held the gun in two hands, one hand wrapped around the other. "Keep your weight low, raise the pistol, sight along the line, okay? Keep the sight just below what you're aiming at. Take a deep breath, let it out. Then *squeeze* the trigger, don't jerk it. Squeeze it so slow you won't even know when it's pulled back far enough to go off. It makes a loud noise—you're not used to it, it can spook you. So . . . put these on." He handed me earmuffs, it looked like. Only the round parts were red. Red plastic, I think. There was foam all around the inside. I fit it over my head. He put one on too, only his earpieces were blue.

I watched the gun in his hands. He walked over, took out a knife, scratched a big X in a tree that was lying on its side. "It's dead," he said. Like he wouldn't shoot a tree that was alive. Then we stepped off about twenty-five feet.

"Watch," he said. He took his stance. I watched his finger move back. There was a crack. It was loud, even with the earmuffs. We walked back over to the tree. You could see the bullet hole just to the right of the X.

"When you use this, you crank them all off. Six shots. Shoot fast. *Empty* the gun. This is a Ruger, Speed Six. Nice, simple piece. It won't jam on you, like an automatic does sometimes. Thirty-eight Special. It'll kill a man, but the more bullets you put into him, the more certain you make it."

He pulled the trigger again. Five times. It sounded like the cracks ran into each other, one loud boom. I saw wood chips fly from the dead tree. We walked back over. The center of the X was all eaten out.

The Indian opened the gun, tipped it back, put the empty bullets in his pocket. "Another thing," he said, "with a revolver, you don't leave cartridges behind at the scene. You use this, you do just what I did, okay? Save the cartridges, dump them someplace else."

"Okay."

"You ready to try it?"

"Yes."

He handed me the gun, six bullets. I did what he did, put them inside. Then I took the same stance he did, crouched there, focusing in on the tree. I took a deep breath, let it out. I could feel my heart beat slower. Slower. I pulled the trigger.

"What are you doing?"

I stopped, turned to him. "What you told me. Pulling it slow."

"Not *that* slow, goddamn it! That trigger was actually moving, that's what you're telling me?"

"Sure."

"How could you tell?"

"I could feel it."

"Damn! Okay, I'm sorry. You got to do it a *little* quicker, okay? You'll be shooting a person, not a damn target. People move."

"You said . . ."

"*Forget* what I said. Try it again, okay?"

I did it again. The first shot made the gun jump in my hands. I fired as it came back down, did it again, picking up the rhythm. Then the gun was empty.

We walked back over. There were more rips in the tree, all around the X.

♣

"He's a natural," a voice said. Another one of the Indians. They must of walked into the clearing while I was shooting.

"I told you," the Indian said.

I practiced some more with the gun. They had all kinds of guns. Rifles, shotguns, a big black pistol that spit bullets out so fast it was like a hose squirting. They worked with the different guns, trading them back and forth. I tried the silver gun in one hand. Then in the other. After a while, it didn't make a difference. It sounded like a war.

Later, one of them brought some sandwiches and cold lemonade. It tasted good. Fresh and clean.

♣

In the afternoon, a woman came into the clearing. An Indian woman, with her hair in braids. She had a bow in her hand. We all sat around while she practiced with the bow and arrows. She was good.

She came over to where I was sitting. Bent down and looked at me. Her eyes were black. Not just the little round part in the center. All black.

"You're the one," she said.

The Indian was next to me. "That's him," he said.

She kept looking at me. "My brother is in their prison," she said. "My own brother. Hiram. From the white man's

Bible, they named him. They separated us, but Hiram came for me. He brought me to my people. Now you will help bring him to me."

Nobody said anything. She held out her hand to me. I took it. Came to my feet, not letting my weight pull against her, but she felt strong enough to do it.

She handed me the bow. "Shall I show you?"

"Yes," I told her. I don't know why I said that.

We walked away from the others. She handed me an arrow. I held it in my hands. It didn't feel right. I shook my head. She smiled, handed me another.

I put it in the bow. I could see how to do it from watching her. She walked away. Pulled a leaf from one of the trees. She licked the back of the leaf, pasted it right over the X the Indian had cut into the dead tree. Then she came back to where I was.

I pulled back the string. I made my left fist into a stone. I pulled all the weight out of my body, put it into my right hand. I could see down the length of the arrow. It was straight. I saw the tip of the arrow, saw the leaf, brought them together. In between my heartbeats, I let the string go.

It went through the middle of the leaf.

The woman bowed her head, like she was in church.

"My name is Ruth," she said.

Then she took the bow from me and walked out of the clearing.

♣

On the drive back to Chicago, the Indian told me how it would work.

"You keep the pistol," he said. "It's ice-cold. Came right off the production line at the factory, never been registered. The way they'll work it, they'll take it from you after the hit. Tell you they're going to get rid of it for you. But they'll keep it. Just in case. It'll have your prints all over it, so they'll always have something on you. You can't wear surgeon's gloves, can't act like a pro around them. You're supposed to be this white-trash nigger-hater, okay? Those kind, they never think things through. You're joining the group 'cause you like to kill niggers, see? Hate's their game. At least that's the game for the troops. The generals, they always have something going on the side."

"What do I do?"

"Do? You don't do nothing. Not for them. You hit one of *our* contracts, see? That's if it works. If they let you go cruising around, tell you to pick a target at random, we can make that work. But if they just *bring* one to you, you got to do it. Just do it. They'll have your prints, so what? Fingerprints don't have a clock on them. You're dead, right? If they threaten you with the prints on the gun, just act scared." He looked at me, watching close. "Can you do that?"

I thought back to the juvenile institution. The training school, they called it. "I think so," I told him.

"From now on, you carry the gun. Don't bother with a holster—just find a comfortable place to carry it. Walk around with it, so the weight goes inside your space, understand? So it don't show . . ."

"Okay."

"They have a joint in Uptown. Not far from us. Just a storefront. They hand out their leaflets, make speeches through bullhorns, crap like that. That's gonna be the hard part for you."

"What?"

"Talking. You watch television?"

"Sometimes."

"Read books?"

"No."

"Okay, no problem. We got a VCR over at the apartment. I'll bring you some tapes. You watch the tapes, you'll see how they talk, what they say. You don't have to be no undercover expert for these boys . . . they got that acid test, like I told you."

"How do I . . . ?"

"You do the *work*. Probably on the street, it all goes down right. Sooner or later, probably sooner, they'll take you inside. To the compound. Take some time, get you alone with the head man. Then you do him. We know where the compound is, but the head man never goes out on the grounds. We watched for a week, once. You get in, we'll be watching. They got all these boys in their camouflage gear on the perimeter. We can go past them anytime we want—they'll never see us. Soon as you do the work, you just step outside. Tie a rag around your head, like this. . . ." He took a red scarf out of his pocket, flipped it into a long, thin piece, tied it around his head. He looked even more like an Indian, the kind you see on TV. "You step out with something around your head, we start shooting. Just run for the perimeter . . . run out of the compound. We'll be there, take you away."

I nodded. I guessed they could just shoot me at the same time, but it didn't feel like that.

"You got any questions for now?" He lit a cigarette, gave me one. I smoked it, thinking.

"That woman, Ruth. The guy who's in Marion, she says that's her brother. Is that her brother like he's *your* brother, or . . ."

"You mean, did they have the same mother and father?"

"Yes."

"They did. But we're all . . . together. The same as blood. Okay?"

"Okay."

We drove for a long time. It got dark out. They never stopped for gas—there was a pump on their farm. The driver kept right around the speed limit, staying with traffic.

"You need ID," the Indian said to me.

"All right."

"The crazy man, he can fix you up with a whole set. And you need a legend too."

"Legend?"

"A history. Like where you came from. I figure, you were in prison, right?"

"Yeah. In Florida."

"What for?"

"Manslaughter."

"Good. Okay, tell them you killed a nigger down there. They'll like that. Tell them as much truth as you can. Whatever name you were under, tell them it was a phony. Your new ID, that'll be the real you. You never said your name."

"My name?"

"What do people call you, friend?"

Monroe called me Ghost. Shella always called me John. Like a joke, her joke. Said I was the only john she ever had. Like I was a trick.

"John," I told him. Thinking about something I saw on TV once. A man signing a motel register. "John Smith," I told him.

One of the Indians in the front seat laughed. It was the first time I realized he'd been listening.

I didn't know what he was laughing at, but it didn't feel like it was me.

The Indian brought me a whole stack of cassettes for the VCR the next day. I watched them over and over again. With the sound on. It was mostly news stories, long ones sometimes. "The Face of Hate," stuff like that. People showing off for cameras, wearing costumes. I'd heard all this stuff before. In prison, there were a couple of guys, in there for killing an old black man. Stomping him to death. Just to be doing it. They had a lot of tattoos. The only one I remember was a spider web on one guy's elbow. When he made a muscle pose, you could see it.

They even had a tape of the head man—the one I was supposed to do my work on. He was giving a speech. Kept talking about race like it was everything. He used dog words. Mongrels, mutts. White people were pure and other people made them dirty, he said. Just being around them would make you dirty.

I heard all that before. Niggers will only fight if they're in a crowd. One-on-one, they're cowards. That's what they told me, the first time I was locked up. I didn't know if it was true. I didn't want to fight anyone—I was afraid of them all. Never hit a nigger in the head—you can't hurt them there. I found out that was a lie. Maybe it was all lies.

"Try and find something in there that's you," the Indian told me.

♣

The Indian brought some more stuff one day, watched the tapes with me for a while. A bunch of college kids raped a black girl. They took turns, and they did it together too. They called her names while they were doing it. One of them made a videotape of it, and the cops found it when they searched the fraternity house. They showed some of it on the news, with pieces of it covered up with black patches, but you could tell what was going on. The girl was all messed up. Drunk, or high. Just sort of laying there.

The college boys said it was a party.

"They say they hate niggers so much, why would they want to have sex with them?" the Indian said. The way people say things when they don't expect you to answer them.

Anyone who's ever been in prison could have told him.

♣

I kept watching the tapes. Watching and listening. One of the shows had interviews with kids. Skinheads. I watched the tape a lot. The older guys, the ones in the organizations, they talked about the skinheads like they were an army.

But the skinheads seemed wild. They were mad at everybody, not just blacks.

Like nobody wanted them, and they knew it.

♣

"What do you see? Just before you go to work on someone, you see anything?"

Nobody had ever asked me that before, not even Shella. I looked at the picture of the head man. The mug shot they gave me. I didn't see anything.

"Not from a picture," the Indian said. "When you're right there."

I closed my eyes, slowed everything down so I could see it. When it happens, it's so fast. I slowed it down. Back to that first time. Duke. He was lying on his back. It was dark in there, but I could see him. I could see . . . his skeleton. Bones underneath his skin. His skull inside his head. "Little dots," I told the Indian.

"Red dots? In front of your eyes? Like when you're mad?"

"Black dots. Not in my eyes. On the body. Not like . . . measles. Just in different spots. All over."

I closed my eyes again. Saw Duke. Touched my face. Between the eyes, the bridge of my nose, a spot on the neck.

"Laser dots," the Indian said.

♣

"You ready to go?" he asked me a few days later.

"Yes."

"Tonight?"

"Sure."

"Okay. I talked to the crazy man. Anybody checks, the guy who did time in Florida was John Smith. It'll all match. We got a room for you. Once you move in, you're on your own—you won't see us again until you finish the work."

♣

He came back that night. I had everything in my duffel bag.

"Let me see the piece," he said.

I handed him the gun. He opened the cylinder, looked down the barrel. "Dusty," he said. He sounded disgusted. He took out a handkerchief, twisted up the corner, poked it through the barrel with a pencil, then pulled it back and forth. "Do that every day, okay?"

I said I would.

They drove me to the Greyhound station. I gave him my car keys. He gave me a ticket stub.

"You came from Atlanta," he told me. "You left around eight in the morning. The trip took about eighteen hours, stopped once in Cincinnati. The ticket cost ninety-eight bucks and change. You got in around two in the morning —just about now. Tonight you stay at this place on Madison. Don't hang around the station—you get picked up with the piece, it's gonna waste a lot of time. Tomorrow, you start out for Uptown. Take the A Train to Sheridan and walk from there. Get a room on Wilson, just off Broadway. It's a wood-frame house, blue front. Then you're on your own."

I stepped out of their car, the duffel bag in one hand. The Indian stepped out with me, watching my face.

"You have money?" he asked me.

I said I did. He held out his hand. I saw, people do that. I held his hand, squeezed when he squeezed.

The Indian shook his head. Sad, like he knew I wasn't going to believe him. "We'll be there when you come out," he said.

♣

I walked through the bus station once, then I came out on Randolph and walked over to the flophouse on Madison. The guy at the front desk looked at me too long—it was good I wouldn't be there past tonight.

Before I went to sleep, I put my handkerchief through the gun barrel a few times.

♣

The next morning, I found the train station, where the Indian said it would be. I took the A Train—it ran outside, above the street. I got off at Sheridan. It was a short walk to the blue house on Wilson. They gave me a room on the top floor. Seventy-five dollars a week.

The room was clean. Even the glass in the window. I looked out. There was an alley back there. An Indian was working on a car with the hood up.

♣

"It's better if you don't just walk in," the Indian had told me. "We'll save that if nothing else works."

When I tried to concentrate on all I had to say, my head hurt. I slept most of the day.

When I woke up, there was a note under my door. The

name of a car wash was printed on it. Underneath it said:
TOMORROW MORNING, GET A JOB.

♣

First thing in the morning, I walked over to the car wash.
An Indian was running it. I asked him for a job. He didn't
ask me anything, not even my name. He pointed to a black
guy, said he was the foreman. I went over to him. He gave
me some towels, told me to wipe down the cars when they
came out of the chute.

I worked all morning. The foreman told me it was lunch-
time. The black guys had a place for themselves in the
back. They all sat down and started to play cards. They
slapped the cards down hard, yelling at each other. They
were playing for money—I saw it on the table. One of them
had a long razor scar down the side of his face. He saw me
looking at him. He looked back—a prison yard stare.

I walked away.

The white guys were by themselves too. Just talking and
eating their food. They had a bottle of wine they were
passing around.

I walked across the street to a deli, got a sandwich and
a bottle of cold water. I sat down next to the car wash.

The Indian boss came by, squatted down next to me. He
spoke without moving his lips.

"Bad enough working with niggers, huh? Having one for
a fucking foreman, that's real hard for a white man to
swallow."

He got up and walked away.

♣

That afternoon, I was wiping down a red Thunderbird. When I finished, the woman got in her car, handed me something. It was two quarters. I put them in my pocket. One of the white guys shook his head, pointed toward a big barrel right next to where the cars came out, a sign on it said TIPS FOR THE MEN.

"We all throw in, split it up at the end of the day," he said.

I threw my two quarters in there.

I finished the shift. We all walked around the back. The Indian came out, gave everyone their pay, in cash. I got twenty-five dollars. Then the black guy, the foreman, he dumped the barrel over. There were a few bills, mostly coins. The black guy counted it up. He split it into two piles, put one pile in his pocket. Then he dealt it out, one coin at a time. He dealt to everyone, all sitting around in a circle. A quarter for one guy, a quarter for the next guy. He started with the first guy to his left. When he came back around to himself, he dealt himself a quarter too. The black guy with the razor scar on his face watched. When he saw the foreman deal himself a share, he put his right hand in his pocket.

I knew what was going to happen. I just didn't know when.

♣

That night, I went to the bar they told me about. It was like all the others, except there was two different flags over the mirror behind the bartender. One was red, with a flat blue X, white stars inside the blue stripes. I saw this flag before, plenty of times, in the South. The Confederate flag, Shella told me it was. The other flag was green on the ends, with white in the middle. The white had a design with horses or something on each side and some other stuff too. I never saw that one before.

I drank the way I always do. Watched the girls. Smoked a few cigarettes. "If nobody comes up to you after a couple of nights, you have to start a talk," the Indian said.

Nobody came near me.

♣

The next night, I was there for a couple of hours when a guy sat next to me. The barmaid came right over, like she knew him, brought him a beer.

He tipped the glass of beer toward me, nodded his head. "Haven't seen you in here before," he said.

"I just got in," I said.

"Where you from?" His accent was like most of the white men in Uptown. Not South, exactly. Harder.

"Florida."

"Looking for work?"

"I got a job."

"Around here?"

"Yeah. In a car wash." I could see the guy didn't know what I was. He wasn't looking for somebody to do work. "Bad enough working with niggers," I said. "Having one for a fucking foreman, that's real hard for a white man to swallow."

"Yeah, that's the way it is now. The fucking apes don't

respect nothing. They're out of control. It's hard to be a white man today. They got all that Affirmative Action shit."

"Yeah." I didn't know what he was talking about. But I felt good inside—I must of gotten it right. I wished the Indian could see me.

"They don't come in here," he said. "They know better."

"Good."

"See that flag?" he said, pointing to the green and white one over the bar. "It's the Rhodesian flag—the true Rhodesian flag, after they kicked out the British. When it used to be a white man's country. Before the nigger-loving UN gave it to the apes. It was a fucking jungle when they started. White men came from England, took it over. Cleared the land. It was a beautiful place. No race mixing, no fucking integration. It was a place for a white man to go, if he had the balls. No matter what your trouble was over here, that was the place to go. Paradise."

"I wish I had known about it," I said.

"You'd go there?"

"It would be better than prison." Telling the truth as much as I could, the way the Indian said.

"You was in prison?"

I gave him a funny look, like you do in there when somebody's close to pushing you.

"Hey, no offense, friend. I been there myself. Armed robbery," he said. Like it was something special. "What'd you go for?"

"I killed a nigger," I told him.

"Is that right? Hey, Katie, bring me another beer. And give my friend here whatever he's drinking. Bring them over to my booth."

♣

The booth was in the back. They're always in the back. A fat guy in a red T-shirt watched us. The way the guy talking to me looked at the fat guy, I could see they were together.

The armed robbery guy did the talking. Nigger this, spic that. "They're really monkeys, you know what I'm saying? You leave them alone, they'd kill each other. Animals. All they want to do is fight and fuck."

I looked at him. He thought I was saying something—his face got a little red. "Hey! Don't get me wrong, pal. I like a good piece of ass better than the next guy. Fucking queers, they're just as bad as niggers, in my book. My point, see, my point is that animals, they need *control*. Like dogs. Dogs are good, they learn to obey, right? Now, niggers, they ain't the real problem. Some people think they're the big problem, they don't know what's going on. You know what the big problem is?"

"What?"

"The Jews, man. The Jews, they're the ones trying to bring the race down. They ain't really white either. I mean, where's Israel? In Africa, am I right? The Jews ain't nothing but Arabs themselves. But you got to give this to the Jews, they're smart. It's in their blood, the way they're bred. A Jew bitch has a retarded kid, you know what they do?" He made a slitting move across his throat.

I looked at him. Every time I did that, he talked more.

"I'm telling you the truth. See, the difference between the Jews and these other beasts, the Jews got a *plan*. Hitler, now he knew what was going on. There's a man who knew the truth. He had the right fucking idea, you know? The ovens."

"The . . . ?"

"Yeah! Exterminate them. That's what has to be done. But the white man in this country, he's lost his balls. This ain't a white man's country anymore—it belongs to the niggers and the Jews."

He talked like that for a long time, until I told him I had to get up in the morning to go to work. "See you tomorrow night?" he said. I told him sure.

When I walked out the door, I could feel somebody behind me. All the way to the house where I had a room.

♣

I went to the car wash the next morning. Just before the lunch break, a car came through. An old Ford station wagon. The guy driving it was the guy from last night, the fat guy. Only he didn't have a red T-shirt.

I didn't show I knew who he was. He didn't leave a tip when we finished wiping down his car.

♣

I went back to the bar that night. This time, I had something to eat. A hamburger and fries. In a booth.

The armed robbery guy came in around nine o'clock. He saw me and came over. Stuck out his hand.

"Hey, partner! Good to see you."

I didn't know what to say so I tried to smile, but I could see that was making him nervous so I said, "Sit down. I'll buy you a beer."

I must of done it right, because he sat down, smiling at me.

While we were waiting for the waitress, he said, "My

name is Mack. Mack Wayne." He stuck out his hand. I took it, squeezed a little softer than he did. He liked that.

"I'm John Smith," I told him.

"Hey, that's funny. I mean, if we took your name and mine, we'd get John Wayne."

I looked at him.

"John Wayne, get it? Like . . . The Duke, right?"

Something moved in me, but I couldn't feel it in my face. "Yeah," I said. "Good."

He drank his beer, talked some more about niggers, queers, and Jews. He said the Jews owned all the newspapers and all the television stations, so the white man never got to hear the truth. Then he said he had to make a phone call.

When he came back, he talked some more about the same stuff. A woman came by our table. A chubby woman with dark hair. She was about thirty-five, in a tight black skirt and high heels, wearing a white sweater with a low neck so you could see the top of her breasts where the bra pushed them together.

"Hey, Ginger!" he said. "Come over here and meet a friend of mine."

He introduced us. Just said my name was John, and we were pals. She sat down, next to me in the booth. Mack ordered some more drinks. Ginger pressed her thigh against me. She had long nails, red. She talked about niggers too—how they all wanted to rape white women and they should be castrated. She had heavy perfume and she stuck her chest out a lot.

After a while, she got up. "I have to go to the little girls' room," she said. She ground her hips hard walking away —she didn't know how to do it the way a dancer does.

Mack leaned over to me. "Hey, pal, I know all the signs. Ginger goes for you. You play your cards right, you could have yourself a nice date tonight."

"Yeah?"

"I guarantee it. I know these girls. I'm gonna take off now, leave you two alone."

I said okay, like it was a good idea.

When she came back, she didn't ask where Mack had gone. She sat across from me. I bought her a couple more beers. She asked a lot of questions, but she wasn't listening much. She was like him—if I looked at her, she got nervous, but if I was quiet, she went ahead and talked.

It was almost eleven when she said she had to be going. "I got to get up early in the morning—I work in a beauty parlor, over on Lawrence."

"I work near there too," I told her.

"You live around here?"

"Just over on Wilson."

"Is it nice?"

"Yeah. I mean, I guess so. It's clean."

"Is it like an apartment or . . . ?"

"Just a room."

"Oh. Well, you know, I was thinking about moving from where I am, finding someplace closer to work. Do you know if they have rooms available?"

"I think so."

"Maybe I could take a look at yours sometime, see how it looks."

"Sure. Anytime you want."

♣

She walked back with me. We went upstairs. She looked all around the room, looked out the window into the alley. I stepped behind her, held her breasts from the underside. She wiggled her butt back against me. She tried to turn around, but I held her there. She didn't fight or anything.

I undressed her, holding her like that. Her breasts were floppy out of the bra. Her thighs were like orange peel when the panty hose rolled down.

I fucked her on her back, her face in my shoulder. When we were done, she lit a cigarette. I laid down next to her and she talked some, asked some questions.

"You don't say much, do you, honey?"

I thought I was making her nervous, so I turned her over on her stomach and fucked her again. It took me longer the second time. She made a little grunting noise just before I finished. Then we fell asleep.

She got up a couple of hours later, moving quiet. I was lying with my head turned to the wall, my face on my arm. I can see good in the dark. She looked through the chest of drawers, at my clothes. Then she went in the closet where I keep the duffel bag. She found the gun. I could see her hold it, looking back at where I was sleeping.

She put the gun back.

Then she got dressed and went out.

♣

The room felt thick in the morning. I opened the window. They still hadn't got that car fixed in the alley.

On my lunch break, the Indian boss walked by. He asked me for a light for his little cigar. When he bent close, he said, "She's with them."

I wanted to tell him I knew that. I'm not stupid because I don't talk. Not stupid like they think. But I didn't say anything.

♣

A couple of nights later, Mack asked me, "You really killed a nigger?"

"Why?"

"No offense, pal. Just, would you mind if we checked you out? I mean, there's a reason, okay? There's people I want you to meet. Important people. Big people. We've got something going, something I know you'd like. But the people in charge, they have to be careful, you understand?"

"I guess."

"Look, what's done is done, right? I mean, you didn't escape or anything . . . ?"

"I got paroled. But . . ."

"Hey, no problem. I know what you're going to say. I'm not a cop. Cops, they're no better than anyone else. Nigger-lovers too, most of them. Even the righteous ones, you got to remember who they work for. . . ."

"The Jews?"

"Yeah! You're getting with the program, John. All right. Listen, all I need is some . . . details. Like where you did time. And when . . . Okay?"

So I told him.

♣

I kept going to the bar. Every night. That woman Ginger didn't come back into the place.

I kept going to the car wash too.

The Indian boss came by one day. When he leaned over to get his light, he said, "There's a basement in your house, where you stay. Go there tonight when you get back from the bar."

♣

There was a guy with Mack that night. A younger guy, a skinhead. He had an earring in one ear, a metal loop, with a little hand grenade dangling from it. Tattoos all over his forearms. He was wearing a leather jacket, jeans, big stomping boots on his feet.

"This is Rusty," Mack said to me.

The skinhead looked hard at me, smiling all across his face so I could see his teeth. "But I ain't rusty, friend. I keep in practice, you get what I mean?"

"No," I told him.

"Johnny ain't no big talker, Rusty. Like I told you. He's a man *does* things."

"Yeah?"

"Yeah!" It was Mack answering the skinhead, not me. We had hamburgers, like always. Mack started talking about the niggers and the Jews. The skinhead, Rusty, he wasn't really listening. He didn't settle in his chair, all bristly, jumpy. He kept staring at me. I looked back sometimes, so he wouldn't think I was afraid. I know his kind —they think you're afraid, they try and hurt you.

"You like to go hunting, man?" he finally asked me.

"I never been," I said.

"*Nigger*-hunting, man. You up for that?"

"Sure."

The skinhead looked over at Mack. He was smiling again.

"Just like that?" he asked me.

"Like what?"

"Go out cruising, spot a nigger, shoot him?"

"Okay."

"*Okay?* Okay, huh? You got any particular . . . preference . . . what kind a nigger you want to shoot?"

I thought about it a minute, trying to get it right. "A fat one," I told him.

Mack laughed so hard he spit up some of his beer.

♣

I could feel him in the basement when I went downstairs that night.

"They're about ready to break," the Indian said.

"They asked me tonight," I told him.

"You know when they want to do it?"

"No."

The glow from his cigarette tip lit his face for a minute. I waited for him to tell me.

"I don't think they got the heart to cruise the South Side, do a drive-by on some gang-banger. But they might. . . . They go that route, you got to do it. Just stick the piece out the window and crank some off. Try to hit some buck flying the colors, okay?"

"I don't . . ."

"One of them in a gang jacket, okay? You've seen them, right?"

"Right."

"Don't spray the stuff around. Make 'em get you close, you understand. You start firing wild, you're liable to take down some kid. . . . Even late at night, they're all over the street."

"Okay."

"I got a better idea. Don't know if we can pull this one off, but it'd be worth it. Come on, let's take a ride."

♣

It was a black four-door Ford. We got in the back seat. A couple of Indians were in the front. I looked close—they were the same ones.

They didn't say anything to me.

"We got a job order," the Indian said. "On a pimp. He works close by, just past Belmont. Runs a string of street girls. He does the gorilla thing, works *little* girls too, understand?"

"Yes." It felt funny to understand what he was saying. I did understand, this time.

"His name is Lamont James, but he goes by Steel. That's what he calls himself, Steel. He's going anyway. You get a chance, do him, it'd be perfect."

I didn't say anything. The Ford turned a corner, doubled back, went around again.

A few minutes later, one of the Indians in the front seat said something I didn't get.

"There he is," the Indian next to me said. "Look at him. Right out of the fifties. Thinks he's Iceberg fucking Slim."

I saw him. A tall, thin man, leaning against the fender of a big pink car with a white padded top. He was wearing a long black coat. He had a white hat too, a big one with a thick pink band.

"You have him?" the Indian asked.

"Yes."

♣

It didn't happen until a couple of nights later. A Thursday night it was. I was talking to Mack in the booth when the skinhead walked in. He had a little baseball bat in one hand.

"Come on out back," he said to me.

When I stepped out into the alley it didn't feel like it had so many times before. I got asked to step out into alleys a lot, and I was always alone when I did. There was a bunch of guys there, all with shaved heads.

"I'll let you know," the skinhead said to Mack. Then he told me, "Come on," and we all walked over to a car. An old white Chrysler.

They showed me where to sit. Next to the window in the back, on the passenger side.

The car started moving, heading south.

The skinhead reached in his jacket, took out a pistol. A big one. He handed it to me.

"I got one," I said, showed it to him.

He slapped hands with the guy in the front seat.

"Let's do it!" he said.

♣

I saw the pink car at the end of the block. A lot of people on the street. I couldn't see him. The Chrysler was moving good—like they had a long way to go.

"There's one," I said.

The guy driving slowed down. "What?"

"A perfect nigger," I told him.

"Where?" Rusty said.

He was just stepping out of the pink car. "There," I told him.

"A pimp," Rusty said. "You wanna do him? It's pretty close to home. . . ."

"Go around the block again," I said.

Rusty rubbed the top of his head. "Do it," he said to the driver.

We came back around, moving slow. "I don't know about this," the guy in the passenger seat said.

I was afraid they'd go someplace else. I wished I could think of something. Then I said, "Stop the car."

They pulled over to the curb.

"Let me out. Keep driving. I'll catch up with you at the end of the block."

Rusty looked at me. Like he never saw me before. Then he nodded. I took out the gun, held it next to my leg— the way the guy with the eyeliner did in the hall when they told me to get out of the rooming house. I opened the door, stepped out. The car moved away.

I walked up the block. The pimp was back against his car, talking to a fat little white girl. He had his hand on the back of her neck. She was wearing a pair of red shorts and a halter top, looked about fifteen.

I walked up real close, people all around. I held the gun up, pointed it at his chest. He saw it. "Hey, man! Don't . . ."

The girl put her hands over her mouth, like trying to stop a scream. I pulled the trigger. It made a loud bang. The pimp grabbed his chest. I put the gun real close to him and kept pulling the trigger. I heard a click, the gun was empty. The pimp was on the ground. People were running around, yelling. I walked away. I can move faster than it looks.

The white Chrysler was at the end of the block. I started running when I saw it. The back door was standing open. I jumped inside.

"Go!" Rusty yelled.

♣

We didn't hear the sirens until we were a couple of blocks away. The Chrysler pulled over to the curb. We all got out, got into another car, a small red one. It was a tight fit in there.

The driver went down by the lake, then he came back, driving slow. They stopped right in front of my house.

"You think you got him?" Rusty asked. "We didn't see nothing, just heard the shots."

"I got him."

"Better give me the gun. We'll get rid of it for you."

"Okay."

"We got one!" the guy in the front said. Like he was surprised. Scared too.

♣

When I walked in the bar Saturday night, Mack had a newspaper in the booth. I sat down next to him. He pointed to something in it.

"Lamont. Ain't that a perfect nigger name?"

"What?"

"The nigger who got it last night. That was his name, Lamont." He was smiling, a big smile, looking at me.

"I didn't know," I told him.

"Oh, man, how *would* you know? Listen, John, you showed me something last night. A lot of guys, they're just talk. Like those boys who took you around . . . ? They're pretty good with baseball bats, doing little 'actions,' they call them, you understand?"

"No."

"Like nigger-stomping, get it? Strike a blow for the race. I mean, lotsa people talk about they going to kill this or kill that, you know what I'm saying? But *doing* it, that's what separates the men from the boys. Like going to prison. You see a lot of guys can't hold themselves together in there, right?"

I nodded.

"Well, it's the same thing. You can't really tell about a man until he has to *do* something. The people I'm with, they do things."

"I thought you said . . ."

"Not those *kids*, Johnny. Men. Men like us. The kids, they're with us all right, but they're not really down for race war. They're like a . . . gang, or something. Not an army. Not professional. They're too wild. You can't count on them. Like the leader says, the niggers got us outnumbered. For now, anyway, until the white race wakes up. So discipline, that's what we need."

He stopped what he was saying when a waitress came close. Ordered some beers. He never did that before, stopped talking.

When the waitress went away, he leaned over close to me. "You like killing niggers, John? Let me tell you something, there's lotsa people feel the way you do. But killing them one at a time, they ain't never gonna get it. The leader says, we kill them one at a time, the fucking monkeys could *breed* faster than we could kill 'em. What we need, what this country needs, is race war. Race *war*. And we got the start of it. Not so far from here. We want you with us, John. And you know what the best part is? You'll be with your *brothers*. Men who'll give their lives for you, go with you to the end. What do you say?"

"I don't get it."

"Look, how'd you like to quit working for niggers over at that car wash? Make some real money?"

"Sure."

"Okay. I got the word. Got it this morning. You got a car?"

"No. All I got . . ."

"That's okay. You had a car, you couldn't bring it anyway. Security don't allow it. Tomorrow night, I'll pick you up myself. Take you to our camp. Then you'll hear what we're about, okay? Make up your own mind. You decide you don't want to be with us, no hard feelings. And I'll guarantee you a month's pay, tide you over until you get another job, if that's what you want. Okay?"

"Okay."

He handed me a bunch of bills. I put them in my pocket.

"Tomorrow night. Ten o'clock. You be out in front of your house."

"Okay, it's over on . . ." I stopped, like I just figured out he must know where I lived. Where they dropped me off last night.

"See, John. We know what we're doing." He winked at me. "See you tomorrow night, brother."

♣

There was a note on my bed. BASEMENT, is all it said. I left the lights on in my room for a while. Then I turned them off like I was going to sleep.

He was there. "Was that enough for them?" he asked me.

"Tomorrow night, they're coming to take me someplace. He gave me some money too."

"I guess that did it. They took the gun from you?"

"Yes."

"Good. Listen to me now. I got to tell you a couple of things. First, don't go to the car wash tomorrow. A guy like you, like you're supposed to be, he wouldn't go to work a car wash job, he had money. What time he's supposed to pick you up?"

"Ten."

"Okay. Stay in tomorrow, like you were sleeping late. Then go out, spend some of that money. Over on Sheridan, they got daytime whores working. Get one of them, spend some money. That's what you'd do."

"All right."

"You have to . . . practice? What you do . . . with your hands?"

"No."

"Good. Now listen. We know where their camp is. We'll be there before you. And we'll be there from then on. Until you come out, okay?"

"Yes."

"I don't know how they work it. Could take weeks before you even see the head man. Or they could take you right

to him, I don't know. We don't know what they do, inside.
Waiting don't bother you, right?"

"No."

"You talk like this when you're around them?"

"Like what?"

"Yes. No. Okay."

"I guess."

"They don't look at you funny?"

"They do all the talking. They like to talk."

His teeth were real white in the basement. "Kill the
niggers, huh?"

"And the others."

"What others?"

"Jews. Spics. Queers."

"No Indians?"

"They never said."

"You understand what they're saying?"

"The niggers are apes. All they want to do is fight and
fuck. Especially fuck white women. Rape them. So the
races get mixed. The white man don't know his true place
in America. This is a white man's country. Like Rhodesia."

He gave me a look.

"Rhodesia's in Africa," I told him. "White men, they built
it right out of the jungle. A long time ago. But the niggers
took it for themselves. And the UN, they didn't do nothing.
What we need is race war. But the white man, he's too
beaten down here. The white man needs to see the light.
So what we need is to start the fighting. Then the white
man will show his true colors."

"Damn! You *listen*, huh?"

It made me feel good, what he said. "I always listen," I
told him.

"So they're going to wipe out all the niggers?"

"That wouldn't do any good," I told him. "They're not the real enemy. They're like dogs—it all depends on who their masters are. The Jews—they're the ones in control. All this stuff, it's part of their plan."

"The Jews, huh?"

"Yes."

"You ever think about that stuff?"

"No."

"Ever kill a Jew?"

"I don't know. . . . how could I tell?"

He made a sound that was like laughing, but kind of strangled. He lit a cigarette, cupping the tip in his hand. Walked around in a little circle.

"You get a chance, ask one of them how it got its name. Rhodesia, okay?"

I nodded, waiting for him to say more.

"You know my name?" he asked.

"Wolf."

"Yes. Listen, now. You get a chance, do him. Don't wait around for the perfect moment—it might not come, okay? You need to be alone with him to do it?"

"It would be better. . . . depends on how many others."

"Yeah. That's what I figured. You remember how to come out?"

"Tie something around my head and run."

"Yeah. You got it."

He didn't say anything for a long time. I waited. He came over, stood real close to me.

"If you think they're on to you . . . if it looks bad . . . just . . . run for it. Don't wait to do him. Run for it. We'll get him some other way."

♣

I stayed in my room the next morning. Lying on my bed with my eyes closed. Like you do in prison. I was watching television. In my head. There's no sound in my head either. I like to watch the nature shows. I look at the ones I saw before.

There was one. A caterpillar. It crawls over a plant, like a bright worm. Eating and eating. Then, one day, it stops. Stuff comes out of it until it's all covered. Then the stuff gets hard. It looks like a jewel, hanging there. A long time passes, and the shell cracks. The shell cracks, and a butterfly comes out.

Then it flies away. I don't know what happens to it after that. When I was a kid, I saw something like that, but I don't remember it so good.

♣

When I got up, it was almost twelve o'clock. I walked over to Sheridan. The whores were out. I saw one, a short blonde in red shorts. For a minute, I thought she was the same one that was with the pimp I killed, but it wasn't her. This one was older.

It was twenty dollars for her, ten for the room. The room was much smaller than mine. A long, narrow room with a bed. There was a paper shade on the window. The sunlight came in. The sheets were gray.

She asked me if I wanted something special. Everybody wants something special. It costs more.

It didn't take long. She cleaned herself off, squatting over a basin on the floor.

She asked me my name, said to come back and see her.
I told her John, and said I would.

I had something to eat in a restaurant. I thought about the
car wash for a minute—it's open on Sundays. You could
work seven days a week if you wanted to, but you had to
work at least five, they said. Walking back to my room, I
saw a blue-and-white police car go by. The cop on the
passenger side gave me a cop look. I looked down—I never
looked back.

I wondered if Shella knew I was coming.

My rent was paid till Monday, so Sunday night was the
right time to go anyway. Maybe they knew that, the people
Mack was with.

I packed my duffel bag. There was plenty of time, so I
watched some more television in my head.

A show about white tigers.

A little black car pulled to the curb. A low, smooth-looking
car. A Firebird, I think. Mack got out of the front seat. He
shook hands with me, opened the trunk, put my duffel bag
in there.

"All set?"

"Sure," I told him.

There was nobody else in the car. He drove on the highway by the lake, heading back downtown.

"We got a ways to go," he said. "Make yourself comfortable. . . . That seat goes all the way back, like an airplane."

I pushed the buttons on the side of the seat until I got it right. I wanted to close my eyes but I thought it would make him nervous.

"How come they call it Rhodesia?" I asked him. "I mean . . . where'd that name come from?"

"From Cecil Rhodes, John. Cecil Rhodes, the Builder of the Empire. He started that country with his own bare hands. You get there first, you're entitled to stamp your name on a country, right?"

"Right."

Two black guys on motorcycles went past us real fast, cutting in and out of traffic. I expected him to say something, but he didn't.

We went back downtown and kept going. We stopped to pay a toll. The signs said we were heading to Indiana.

He was smoking a lot. I felt like I should say something, but I didn't know how.

We turned off the highway. There was a sign, but all I could see on it was South and some number.

He drove careful, not too fast.

"Could you use a beer, Johnny?"

I told him sure.

♣

When we got back on the road, the clock on the dashboard said 12:45.

"You have any questions?"

"When does it start?"

"What?"

"The race war?"

He turned sideways to look at me. His face was a little sad. I never saw him look like that before.

"This is a military operation, John. We're a guerrilla force. . . . You know what that is?"

"No."

"Like . . . we hide in the jungle, then we sneak out and zap them and sneak back. See what I mean? We don't have enough manpower to just march in and take over. It's our job to start the fire. First it gets going strong enough by itself, then we provide the leadership. When the white man rises up angry, he's not going to know what to do. The Jews, they've been running the government so long, the white man's forgot how to do it. That's where we come in."

"Where?"

"We all got our jobs. Those boys you went out with, we got people who work with them. They're the shock troops. They keep the action going. Heighten the contradictions, that's what the leader taught us. I don't work with them myself. Me, I'm in recruitment."

"Recruitment?"

"Sure. That's one of the most delicate jobs of all. I have to, like . . . screen the applicants. My judgment is very important. I started out just bringing guys in. At the plant where I worked. I put in a long time doing that. When I'd find a right guy, I'd turn him over to one of the coordinators—the guys who run the individual groups. And I worked my way up. What I do now, I recruit for the cells."

"The cells? Like in . . . ?"

"No. A cell is a small group. It operates all by itself. With specific targets. We got procurement cells . . . they raise money for our treasury. I recruited for them. You're my first recruit for the Lightning Squadron."

"What's that?"

"Doing what you did Friday night."

"Killing niggers?"

"Killing whoever. Like I told you, it's not niggers we're worried about."

"Killing Jews?"

"Whoever. Any enemy of the race. There's plenty of white men who're enemies of the race too. Traitors."

"That's what I'll do?"

"Yeah. I seen other guys from the Lightning Squadron, but I never brought one in myself before. I'm supposed to look for guys. For different things we need. But as soon as I met you, I said to myself, there's a man for the squad. It's a real honor, Johnny. For me too, I want you to know. I passed your name on to HQ, and they checked you out."

"HQ?"

"Headquarters. They got an Intelligence Unit. You wouldn't believe the places we got people. See, the Jews are clever, Johnny. They're always trying to infiltrate our operations. So we got to be sure who we're dealing with. They checked your record. We got other ways too. Remember Ginger?"

"Sure."

"She's one of us."

"Ginger?"

He smiled, looking out the windshield. "Yeah, sure. It's not just men in with us. Women. Kids too."

"The skinheads, right?"

"No, I mean *little* kids. We raise them right, in the white man's way. The leader says they're the hope of the future, the kids. We got kids eight years old, know more about their true heritage than the average grown man could ever imagine. Anyway, a man's gonna be considered for the squad, we got to test him. The acid test, we call it. Mostly, unless the man has got a name for himself, like if he was with us inside, we bring him out, give him the test. This time, the leader told me, test this guy outside. We got to be careful, can't be bringing too many guys inside. In case they don't pass the test, see?"

"I guess so."

"Johnny, listen to me a minute. These are serious people I'm taking you to. You can't fuck with them. These men will be your brothers. And that's forever. This ain't something you can get tired of, go on to something else. Your brothers, you know what that means?"

"They're all white?"

"Yeah, of *course* they're all white, for Christ's sake. That's not what I mean. Brothers. Like *blood* brothers. This is for a cause, Johnny. A holy cause. You'll see, inside. When they show you right in the Bible. This is bigger than any of us. No matter where you go, your brothers will be around. Even in prison. You'll never be alone."

I guess he meant it to be a threat, but it sounded like it was a good thing, the way he said it.

"It's on me, I bring a man in. You do good, it'll be on me. You fuck up, it'll be on me too."

"I won't fuck up," I told him.

He put his hand on my shoulder, squeezed it hard.

♣

We drove for a long time. The roads kept getting smaller. He never checked directions or anything. We were outside the cities. Just a farmhouse once in a while. The clock said 2:12.

It was still dark when he turned off onto a dirt road.

"We have to go slow from here," he said. "The first checkpoints won't stop us—they're just watchers."

I didn't say anything.

There was a telephone between the two front seats. He picked it up, pushed in a number.

"It's me," he said. "I just passed checkpoint three. I've got him with me."

He listened for a minute, then he put the phone back.

♣

We came around a bend in the road and there was a log lying across it on an angle. We couldn't drive past. Mack stopped the car. Spotlights came out of the night—little ones, slicing across each other.

Men came out of the woods. They were dressed like soldiers, in those suits that look like the woods, green and brown. They all had guns.

Mack told me to get out of the car. He did too. One of the soldiers patted my clothes. Then he told me to take my jacket off and my shirt too. Mack said it was okay. They didn't ask him to do it.

"No wire," one of the soldiers said.

"All the way," another said to him.

The first soldier told me to take all my clothes off, even my shoes and socks. I did it. It was cold out there.

Another soldier stepped over to me. He was putting a rubber glove on his hand. "Bend over and spread 'em," he said. "Just like in the joint."

I did it. He was rough with his finger. When he took it out, he pulled off the rubber glove, threw it away in the woods.

"Okay, get dressed," the first soldier said to me.

Another one had my duffel bag on the ground. They took everything out, piece by piece, going over it.

"It's clean," one of them said.

Mack came over to me, held out his hand. "They'll take you the rest of the way, Johnny. You're gonna see things you never dreamed of. I know you're gonna make me proud of you. Proud that I brought you in."

"You're not coming?" I asked him.

"No. I won't see you again, not for a while. Maybe never. It depends."

"Goodbye, Mack," I said.

"Goodbye, brother," he said, turning away.

♣

On the other side of the log, they had a pickup truck and a couple of Jeeps. They had those bars that run over the top of the cabs, all with lights on them. I got in where they told me, and they chased each other going back. It made a lot of noise.

From the way they were dressed, I thought they would live in tents. But it was all buildings, like a little town. I couldn't see much—it was still dark. They put me in a big room with bunks in rows. Like the juvenile institution they put me in once. Only there was no bars on the windows.

♣

I got up when it turned light in the morning. There was only two other guys sleeping in the dorm where I was. Neither one moved when I got up.

My duffel bag was at the foot of my bunk. I took it into the shower room, got cleaned up, changed my clothes. Still nobody came around.

I went outside and sat down on the steps. I had a cigarette. It was quiet, like being around a bunch of drunks sleeping it off.

I wondered if everybody was sleeping. If the smiling man in the mug shot was sleeping real close to me, someplace.

I didn't try and figure out what to do. Shella told me once she danced because she was good at it. I told her she was good at a lot of things, she could do them too. She said that was sweet, for me to say it. And she gave me a kiss. Like a kid does, maybe. On the cheek. She told me I was good at different things too. I knew the one thing I was good at, so I asked her, "What else?" She looked at me a long time. I didn't move, just watched her watch me. Finally, she came over, sat next to me. "Waiting," she said. "That's what you're good at, honey. Waiting."

♣

A guy with a beard and a watermelon belly walked past where I was sitting. "They serving breakfast yet?" he asked me. I told him I didn't know. "Come on, let's take a look," he said. I got up and walked with him.

It was the next building. Like a cafeteria, except that the tables were all scattered around and the food wasn't already cooked.

The woman behind the little counter was skinny. She looked real tired. The place was almost empty—I only saw a couple of guys, eating in one corner.

"You got pancakes this morning, Flo?" the fat man asked her.

"I didn't make up the batter yet," she said. "How about some bacon and eggs?"

"Suits me," he told her. "What about you, friend?"

I said that would be good. I didn't see any cash register and I couldn't tell what things cost. We sat down at one of the tables. When the food was cooked, the woman behind the counter said it was ready and we went over and got it.

In the middle of eating, the fat man told me his name was Bobby. I told him my name and we shook hands. The other guys who were there, at the other table, when they got finished eating, they picked up their plates and brought them over to the counter. The waitress took them and put them in a big rubber bin.

Bobby took out a pack of cigarettes, asked me if I wanted one. I said thanks.

"When'd you get in?" he said.

"Last night."

"Yeah, I heard a new man was coming. Who brought you in?"

"They didn't tell me their names," I said. "A bunch of guys."

"Oh, you mean the transport team. No, I mean, who was your recruiter?"

I looked at him.

"Your recruiter, man . . . the guy who talked to you about—"

"He knows what you mean." A voice behind me. I didn't recognize it. When he stepped around, I could see it was one of the soldiers from last night. A short man wearing a black T-shirt. His arms were big, like he lifted a lot of weights. "See, Bobby, this man, he just got here. And he already knows more than some of the veterans. Like how to keep his mouth shut, see?"

"Hey, don't get your balls in an uproar, all right, Murray? I was just being friendly, a new man and all."

Murray introduced himself, sticking out his hand. He put a lot of pressure into the grip. "Flo take care of you all right?" he asked me.

"Sure."

"Okay. You all finished? Good. I'm gonna take you to meet some people."

I took my plates over to the counter. When the woman came over, I told her, "It was good. Thanks." She gave me a funny look.

♣

It was wide daylight now, and I could see everything as I walked across the compound with Murray. It wasn't all that much, not as big as it looked at night. Most of the buildings were like houses; only one was higher than the first floor.

You could walk to anyplace they had. The front was open. Across the back, there was this high fence, but it didn't connect to anything. Like they started it and never got it done. Murray saw me looking at it.

"When it's finished, the whole compound'll be behind a

wall. That's just the preliminary work you see there. This is all our land. We own it. Free and clear, and all legal. Five thousand acres . . . a lot more than you see here. All the woods around here, even the road you came in on, it's all ours. That's one thing the leader taught us, to own our own. Own our own. There's no welfare in here, no government, no IRS, no nothing. On our land, we make all the rules. You want to live pure, you want your kids to be raised pure, you got to own your own to do it."

I nodded the way I always do when I don't understand something. He kept showing me things, saying how they owned it all.

We came to this house at the back, near that fence they were building. Murray knocked on the door. The guy who answered it was wearing a shoulder holster like he was used to it. He turned his back and we followed him. It looked like a regular house, living room and kitchen and all. We walked past, to the back, where the bedrooms would be. It was a much bigger room than I thought, bigger than the living room. A man was sitting behind this desk they made out of a door laid flat across a pair of sawhorses. The walls were covered with maps, colored pins stuck in them.

The guy behind the desk was wearing a white shirt and a dark tie. He had glasses, and he looked older than the others, but maybe that was because he was losing his hair in front and he combed it over from the side. That always makes you look older.

The guy with the shoulder holster said, "Thanks, Murray," and Murray got a look on his face like he wasn't happy about the way the guy said it, but he didn't say anything himself before he walked out.

The guy in the shoulder holster told me to have a seat,

pointing with his finger for me to sit on the other side of the desk from the guy in the white shirt.

I sat there and waited.

♣

The guy in the white shirt studied me. I couldn't figure out if I was supposed to be nervous, so I lit a cigarette like I needed something to do. I guess it was a good idea, because the guy in the shoulder holster lit one too.

The guy in the white shirt was looking at his fingernails. "What'd you kill the nigger with?" he asked me.

"I shot him," I said.

"Not *that* nigger, the one in Florida."

I remembered the Indian, telling me to stay right next to the truth as much as I could. The lawyer they got to throw me away in Florida, I remember him asking me where the weapon was . . . what I had killed the guy with. They just had "blunt object" on the police report, the lawyer said, and it would be better if I told them where the weapon was. So I knew the answer. "A tire iron," I told the man in the white shirt.

"Why?"

" 'Cause it was right there."

"Not why you used a tire iron," he said. He was using that tone people use when they talk to me sometimes—like I'm stupid and they're being nice about it but it's hard work. "Why did you kill him in the first place?"

"I was in this motel," I told him. "He had a white woman in his room with him. I saw her leave. I said something to him and he said something back. The next thing I know, it was done."

"You lost your temper?"

"I guess. . . ."

"You hate niggers?"

"Yes."

"How come?"

"How come?"

"Yeah. How come. How come you hate them?"

" 'Cause . . ." I tried to think of all the stuff Mack told me—it all got mixed in my head. I knew they'd think I was stupid. "'Cause . . . if it wasn't for them, this would be a good place."

"What place?"

"America. Our country. It would be a good place without the niggers. They're dirty animals. And all the government wants to do is make them happy."

"The Jew government," the guy in the shoulder holster said.

I nodded. The guy in the white shirt gave the other one a look, like he shouldn't help me with the answers.

"You want a pure race?" he asked me. "A pure white race?"

"Yes."

"Are you willing to do battle for your race?"

"Yes."

He leaned back in his chair, rubbing his chin like he was considering something.

"You a pretty good shot?" he asked me.

"If I get close enough."

They both laughed, but it sounded like they thought I said the right answer.

♣

They gave me a lot of stuff to read. Piles of it. Books and magazines and little thin things with covers. I took it all back to the dorm.

I tried to read the stuff. I don't read so good, but I know how.

They had a television in the dorm. I was watching it one day when the guy in the white shirt came in. He asked me why I had it on with the sound off. I told him I was trying to read the books he gave me. He looked at me for a minute, then he said "Good," and walked out.

♣

There were always people around, but I was by myself. Like prison. Like being out of prison too, when I thought about it. I thought about it. I thought about what people say in prison, how you have to kill time. They would do all these things . . . basketball, dominos, read magazines. To make time pass. They thought I was stupid because I didn't do anything. To make time pass. I'm not stupid. Not like they think, anyway. Time passes by itself—you don't have to do anything.

It is different, though, prison. Being inside, you don't work. When I was outside, before Tampa, I was with Shella. I didn't think about her—she was there. When I was inside, I would think about her. Like studying. But all I ever figured out was that Shella had the answers, not me.

I thought about her a lot in the compound. No dreaming—I wasn't asleep when I did it. Shella had bad dreams sometimes. She woke up once, making noises like she couldn't breathe. I grabbed her—she was strong. When it was over, my shoulder was bleeding. From where she bit me. She was sorry, sad about that. She poured some stuff on where she bit me.

She wanted to tell me what was in her bad dream, but when she started to tell me about the broomstick, I got sick and she stopped.

"Don't you ever have dreams, honey?" she asked me.

I never thought about it before that. I guess I don't.

♣

Shella liked to dress up. She had all kinds of clothes. She even had eyeglasses she wore sometimes. I put them on once—they were just plain glass. She wore them when she put her hair on top of her head, when she went out some-times, all dressed up like an older lady.

She didn't wear the glasses for reading. Shella read all the time. I asked her to read some of it to me once, but I couldn't understand the words. It wasn't like the stories. After a while, I fell asleep.

♣

One time when Shella got her period, she had terrible cramps. They hurt so bad she cried. I didn't know what to do. I got a cold washcloth, tried to put it on her head. She threw the washcloth at me. "It's my guts that hurt, not my head, you stupid bastard!" she yelled. But when I put on some of the music she liked, she said it gave her a headache.

I asked her if she wanted a cigarette. A drink, maybe?

She was curled up in a little ball then, holding her stomach. When I touched her back, it was like iron.

It hurt me to hear her cry like that. I filled the bathtub with hot water. The bathroom got all steamy. I put some of the green bubble stuff she liked in there. I pulled her robe off. Then I picked her up in that ball she was wrapped in and carried her inside. I lowered her into the tub. She tried to bite me, but I held her face hard against my chest until I got her in.

"It's too hot," she said, but I kept her there.

She came out of the ball and laid back. I held the back of her neck so she wouldn't go under.

"The water's all turning red," she said, real quiet.

After a while, she started to cry again. But it was different, the crying. I let the water out of the tub. Then I stood her up against me and showered her off. All the bubbles and the blood ran down the drain.

She was still crying when I dried her off. I took her into the bedroom and put her on the bed.

"Could I have powder?" she said.

I knew the powder. Baby powder. Shella always puts it on under her pants. I spilled some on her. "That's too much," she laughed. A little laugh, like a giggle. But she wasn't crying by then. I rubbed it all over her. Then she rolled over and I did it on her back too. On her bottom and legs too. Then I covered her with some sheets and she fell asleep.

It was dark when she woke up. I was in the chair, next to the bed. I patted her. She took my hand and kissed it. "I'll make it up to you, baby," she said. Then she went back to sleep.

♣

I don't dream, but I can see things, like on a screen if I close my eyes. I did that in the compound. A lot, sometimes for a whole day. I would think about why I was there, and then it would start. Shella.

A couple of nights after she had the cramps, Shella came in and took a shower. She was in there a long time. When she came out, she was naked. I was on the bed, watching TV. Shella turned it off. It was dark in the room, but I could see good. The neon sign outside the motel flashed off and on against Shella's body. She was red, then she was blue.

"Do you want a cigarette?" she said.

I told her okay, and she lit one for me. Then she crawled onto the bed on her hands and knees, watching me. She licked me a couple of times and I got hard.

"You want something special?" she asked me.

"What?"

"*Special*," she whispered. "Like you haven't had before."

I knew she meant sex. I closed my eyes, thinking. I dragged on the cigarette until it was done.

"You can't think of anything, can you?" Shella was still whispering. "Nothing you want you didn't already have, huh, baby?"

"Anything is . . . I mean, anything you . . ."

"Ssssh, baby. I know. I was thinking too. Special. Like something I never did with anyone else, you know?"

"Yes."

"But I couldn't think of anything I haven't done," she said. She lay down on my chest. Her body was shaking.

Her hands dug into me. I could feel wet on my chest but I couldn't hear her cry.

♣

Nothing much happened where I was. People came in and out all the time, and you could tell some things were going on in other parts of the place. There was a lot of practice with guns. I did that too. I didn't know anything about the guns, but they showed me. The guy who showed me, he liked to do that. He was glad I didn't know anything so he could teach me. He was a good teacher— he wanted to make people smart, not tell them they were stupid.

The targets were pictures of people. Some were famous people. Some were just different kinds of people. Black people were their favorite.

Gunfire was always going on.

♣

They had classes in other things. Political classes. And fighting too. One teacher, he was dressed all in black, even with a hood over his face. He said he was a ninja. He mostly talked.

Every time he would ask for a volunteer, I would sit very still. I was scared to do this. But one day he made me. He told me to come up behind him and get him in a choke hold, try and pull him down.

I was so afraid I'd break his neck that I grabbed him around the jaw instead of the throat. He hit me hard in the ribs with an elbow and then chopped me in the neck. It hurt, where he hit me.

He told me to stick with guns. Some of them laughed.

♣

I was there about two weeks when Murray told me the leader was going to talk the next morning.

Everybody in the whole camp was there. In a big hall in the back, with the doors open.

He was the man in the mug shots. The same man. He was a good talker. There must have been a couple of hundred people in the room, but he didn't use a microphone and he didn't shout.

It was a good speech. He said we were the warriors. The warriors of the right. Not the right wing, he said, the right way. Mostly he talked about race. Pure races. How they got all mixed together. Like dogs. Mongrel dogs. He said our race was like snow on the ground, covering the dirt underneath. When the snow melts, it could wash all the dirt away. But if you mix stuff in with the snow, it gets all filthy. It's not beautiful anymore. Not pure.

He said niggers weren't the real enemy. It was the Jews. It's the Jews who gave us the niggers. The Jews needed animals to work the land around Israel—that's where Israel is, Africa. So they started experimenting with different animals. They are real fine scientists. And that's how they ended up with niggers, like a cross between apes and people. The niggers are just animals—they were being used by the Jews. He said even the stupidest niggers were waking up to this. Niggers in the big cities hate the Jews too. He said they were getting smarter to be feeling that way.

That's what comes of educating niggers. He said the Jews hate themselves because they really want to be white. He said the big Jews are born smart, but the regular Jews, they're always trying to be friends with the niggers.

The leader said that our race was dying. The niggers and the Jews breed faster than we do. Soon there would be more of them than us. And that would be the end. He said white men have always known this, but we always got ruined by fighting among ourselves. That's what he said. He said there were a lot of white-power movements, but they always fought each other.

He said he would give examples. He said that Europe was all white men. Nothing but white men. If white men fight white men, white men have got to lose. He said that over and over again.

He had a Bible with him, and he talked about what was in it. He talked about resources—he said that a lot, resources. How if we had enough resources we could have our homeland.

"Partition!" he yelled. And everybody cheered.

He said Partition was our own land. A couple of states for white people only. Our own schools, our own churches, everything our own.

The Promised Land, he said it like it was holy. He said it was promised to us, right from the Bible. The truth of God.

God was a white man, everybody knows that. Even the niggers know that. That's why they hate us.

He talked for a long time. When he was done, everybody yelled. Some of them waved guns in the air.

♣

Everybody talked like the leader, but he was the best at
it. I practiced with the guns they had. I read the stuff they
gave me. They watched TV a lot—they never watched the
nature shows. They played cards a lot. Mostly, they just
worked, like anyplace else. Cooking, cleaning, fixing. Some
of them, they would just come and go.

Everybody called everybody brother in there. Everybody did it. I never heard white people do that before I
went to prison the first time.

They never seemed to go out in the woods, but they
were always dressed for it.

Murray came by the dorm one morning. He walked over
to my bunk, sat down on the next one. I was glad I had
some of the reading in front of me.

"How come you don't put up no pictures?" he asked me.

I didn't know what to say. I used to hate that, before I
figured out I didn't have to say anything. But that was for
other places. I looked around the big room. Guys had pictures on the walls near where they slept. Mostly women.
From magazines. Their favorites were women wearing soldier stuff, like a naked girl with a rifle. I don't understand
pictures, why people have them. I mean, maybe a picture
of a real person, to remember them. But men who buy
magazines, they don't know those women. Shella tried to
explain it to me once, but I stopped listening once she got
crazy. When Shella talks about why men do things with
women, she gets twisted up inside and scary. I couldn't
think of anything to say to Murray so I just shrugged. He
gave me a look, like he knew something about me. I saw

the muscles flex hard across his arm as he looked at me.

I seen that kind of look all my life.

♣

Murray came by where I was a lot. I got used to seeing him. One night, he just looked in the door. "Come on," he said. "Cadre meeting."

I got up and went outside with him. I followed him, walking across the compound. He was almost bouncing, he was so pumped up, humming to himself, clenching his fists.

Inside the room where he took us there was maybe eight, ten guys. Nobody was saying much, just smoking and standing around.

The guy in the white shirt came in the back door, turned an easy chair so it was facing us, and then he went and stood in the corner.

The leader came in and sat down. He had a suit on with a white shirt but no tie. He looked like the mug shot, just like it. Everybody stood up when he walked in. Then he made some gesture with his hand, like waving, and everybody sat down. I was the last one to sit, because I didn't know what to do. And the guy in the white shirt, he never sat down.

"I just wanted to walk in here and tell you, again, how much the Nation values your sacrifices. I know it's no fun, giving up what you did, making those sacrifices. Like the good book says, if there's a reason, there's a season. There's a time for everything. Soldiers make sacrifices . . . that's the way of the warrior. But tonight, you're getting a little break. Not the whole camp, now, just this cadre. What we're going to have is a little training exercise, a full-dress rehearsal. Some of you have already been blooded, some of you haven't gone the distance. Tonight isn't that. Tonight's just a way of spreading our message. Any questions?"

Nobody said anything. I was toward the back of the room, but I could feel people behind me.

The leader looked all around the room. He had a way of looking you in the face that didn't challenge you. Not trying to stare you down, just making sure you was listening to him. You could look back at him and it wasn't the signal to fight.

"Being a Christian doesn't mean you don't have anything to do with sex," he said to us. "A man is going to want sex, that's the way nature intended it. But in these times, a man has to be careful. There's a lot of traps out there."

He took a pipe out of his shirt pocket. A white pipe with a yellow stem. He pushed down the tobacco with his thumb, fired a wooden match, and took his time getting it going. Nobody else lit up. When he got it going, he took a puff. Then he held the pipe in his hand, looking at it, just settling down.

"You men are going to have a little party tonight. Just down the road, about an hour's drive from here, there's a little prostitution ring operating. They've got three trailers parked side-by-side in this spot out behind a tavern, back in the woods, where you can't see them from the road. Billy knows where it is—he'll be leading the convoy.

"Now let me tell you a little bit about this operation. It's run by white men, but they don't act like it. They don't serve niggers in the roadhouse, but out back, they get the same rights as white men. You understand what I'm saying to you, boys? You fuck one of those trailer whores, and you may be going in right behind a nigger. You may be pulling

sloppy seconds after a jungle bunny. Now, we *told* the guy
who runs the operation we wouldn't stand for this. Explained it to him real clear. He said he was gonna set up
a separate trailer for them, and we went along. But we sent
our own people in, and you know what they told us . . . ?
The niggers can only go in the trailer on the left, but the
girls, they go to all of them. They're on rotation, you see
what I'm saying?"

Some of the men nodded. I just watched him. He was
too smart—there had to be more.

"Anybody here know how to make a good fire?" The
leader looked around the room.

One guy raised his hand. I could see from his face that
he knew all about fires. The leader looked across at the
guy in the white shirt. They kind of nodded to each
other.

"Okay," the leader said. "We got a rifleman here too?"

Three of the guys put their hands up. The leader looked
at the closest one, a guy with long blond hair and a mus-
tache. "Where'd you learn?"

"I was in the 'Nam," the blond guy said.

"Good enough, brother. What about you?" He was asking
another guy, a guy with a shaved head.

"Prison guard," the man said.

The leader moved his eyes to the third man. He was
bigger than the others, with his hair combed forward over
his eyes, like bangs. "Hunting . . ." he said. Like he was
ashamed of it.

The leader kept asking questions. He had a soft, friendly
voice. Everybody liked him, you could see it.

"No reason why you can't have a little taste before you
get to work. Thing is, with whores, you got to be careful.
A whore is a liar, always remember that, men. A whore is

a liar. Lying is their trade. Lying on their backs, lying with their mouths. So you have to watch yourselves at all times, be careful you don't get something you didn't bargain for. Everybody know what I mean?"

Everybody nodded. Somebody said "Yeah," but so soft I couldn't tell who it was.

"Is that right?" the leader said. "You all know what I mean, huh? Well, okay, how about *you* tell me what I mean." He pointed at a guy right across from me. A bloaty-looking guy with real hairy arms.

"Don't go out without your rubbers. . . . I mean, don't go in without them," the fat guy said. On his face was a look like he got the right answer.

A couple of men laughed, but they stopped when the leader looked at them.

"Yes, that's certainly true," he said. "But I'm thinking of something else. Some of these little girls, well, they're not girls at all. Understand?" He looked around the room. "Now, who knows how you tell whether you're looking at a real woman, or one of those transvestites . . . a homo-sex-ual dressed up like a woman?"

Nobody said anything. Nobody knew the answer.

I knew.

I knew the right answer.

I raised my hand. The leader nodded at me. I touched my Adam's apple. The leader smiled. "Now, where'd you learn that, son?"

I didn't know what to say. I didn't know why I raised my hand. I was stupid, that's why I did it. I couldn't tell him about Shella, how I learned those things, where I'd been. I felt myself being pushed in, like the air was too heavy. I didn't know what to say.

"In prison," I said.

The leader sort of chuckled. "Yes, that's been the graduate education for many of us, hasn't it? Well, you're right. Right on the money."

He bowed his head, like he was praying. I saw the others do it, so I did it too.

The man in the white shirt, he kept watching us.

♣

After the leader left, the man in the white shirt took out a clipboard. He wrote something on it, then he kind of pointed at the guy who was with him the first time I saw him. The guy with the shoulder holster.

That guy explained what we were going to do. Some of the guys asked questions—you could see it was okay to do that with the leader out of the room. The way they talked about it, it was like this army thing.

But what they were going to do, it sounded like the same way they send a message in the city.

♣

We went in three cars. I was in the back of a station wagon, Murray was next to me. He kept squeezing a set of those handgrips, the ones with springs, to make you stronger. Over and over, switching them from one hand to the other. The handles were red, wood.

They had asked me what kind of gun I wanted—they had a whole bunch of them spread out on a table. I took one that looked like the one the Indian gave me.

The roadhouse was like a long, dark diner. Neon sign

outside: Rebel Inn. The parking lot had mostly pickup trucks in it. You had to walk this dirt path around the back to get to the trailers.

There were three of them, like the leader said, one standing off by itself to the left.

"Twenty-two hundred hours, right on target," one of the men said. The guy in the white shirt had said we should be there by ten o'clock, but I didn't say anything.

The three guys with the rifles went in first. We had to wait for them to finish so they could stand guard. It didn't take long. We all got a turn. I knocked on the door to the trailer. A skinny old woman with a big blonde wig let me in. It cost thirty bucks. The room was like a closet. The girl in there was tired and she smelled bad. You could hear the people grunting in the next room over—the walls were made of some cardboard stuff. I finished quick.

When we got together outside in the parking lot, the one they called Billy checked us over. He pointed to the house on the left, told me and Murray to take that one. The other ones fanned out.

"You see one, shoot him," Murray said. "They all carry razors and they'll cut you in a minute."

"Okay," I said.

Murray knocked on the door. A woman in a red dress opened it—she was fatter than the door opening. We climbed up the steps and went inside. We took out our guns.

"Get your hands up," Murray told the fat woman.

She did it. She looked bored.

"How many girls you got back there?" he asked her.

"Three."

"They all busy?"

"Two are. Mary's alone in her room."

"Where's the phone?"

"There's no phone here. We use the one in the tavern." The fat woman sat down, lit a cigarette. Murray looked mad, but he didn't say anything.

The fat woman dragged on her cigarette. I could hear a radio playing. Country music, it sounded like.

"Call her out . . . this Mary. Get her out here."

The fat woman started to get up, then she sort of shrugged, yelled "Maaary!"

Another fat girl came out, this one was younger. She was wearing a shortie nightgown and high heels. When she saw the guns, she went and sat down next to the other one, like she was half asleep.

"You try to run, I'll blow you away," Murray said to the women. They didn't look like they could.

The hall was too narrow for two of us. Murray went first. He stood outside a door to the left, pointed to my door on the right. He stepped back and kicked the door. It made a loud noise but it held. He kicked it again. I heard a scream. I turned the handle of my door and it opened. Inside there was a man just getting off a woman. They were both naked, except he had socks on. I pointed the gun at them.

"Get out," I said.

The man kind of jumped into his pants, grabbed up his clothes and ran out. The woman just laid there.

"There's gonna be a fire," I told her. I walked out of the room and I heard a shot. I looked through the open door. Murray was aiming at a man—I couldn't tell if he hit him or not.

"Come on," I yelled at him. "It's going up."

He followed me out. The two fat women were still sitting in the front room.

Another shot, from one of the other trailers. A man in a red jacket came in the front door. He had a stocking mask over his face and a metal gasoline can in one hand. He started splashing the gasoline all over—the smell was choking me.

The two fat women ran out. When the fire man got to the back of the trailer, the other two women came out too.

We went back to the parking lot. There was a big *whooosh!* from between the three trailers. A fireball went up, then it shot out in three arms. You could see it rip toward the trailers. They all went up. It sounded like a war . . . explosions from inside, popping, then a big bang. People were running out of the tavern. There was a lot of shooting, but it was all up in the air. Two men ran to a corner of the parking lot. They stuck a cross in the ground. The guy in the red jacket lit that too.

That was all. We got in the cars and took off. Nobody tried to stop us. I couldn't hear sirens.

♣

The car I was in had a police radio in the front seat. I couldn't understand it with all the crackling, but the guy next to the driver said the State Police were rolling toward the tavern. By then we were miles away.

When we got back, they dropped us off near the dorms. The guy in the shoulder holster was waiting. He told me and Murray to come with him.

We walked to another building, where the guy in the white shirt was waiting.

Murray went in first. The guy with the shoulder holster told me to wait.

When it was my turn, the guy in the white shirt asked me what happened. I told him.

"Good work," he said.

♣

I was walking back when I saw Murray ahead of me. He must have been waiting—I was in with the man in the white shirt for a while.

"What'd you tell him?" Murray asked me.

"What happened."

"About the niggers?"

"What niggers?"

"At the place . . . the niggers. I told him I . . . shot one. A nigger. In the room with a white girl."

I didn't say anything. All the men in the house had been white.

Murray put his hand on my arm. I let him do that—he was scared of something.

"John, did he ask you . . . if there was any niggers there?"

"No."

"You won't tell . . ."

"Tell what?"

"You're my true brother, John," Murray said, squeezing my arm hard.

♣

On the TV the next day, they said it was the KKK who set fire to the trailers. Some of the guys watching cheered.

The fire man rubbed his hands, watching the tape of the burning.

♣

It was another ten days or so when Murray came by. All excited again. Worked up.

"We going to an Action Team, John. I just heard. They tell you yet?"

"No."

"Hey, it's true. I got it straight from HQ. You'll see, both of us got tapped."

He was pacing around in a little circle, really happy.

The only thing I knew about the Action Team was what the leader said in one of his talks. He talked about Partition again. He said the niggers wanted their own land too, but, like all niggers, they wanted the government to just give it to them. Like Welfare. Our land, he said, our land would come from our own labor. We would pay for it. The Action Teams, they were the way they got the money.

♣

The guy in the white shirt, he was the one who told us about the Action Team they picked me and Murray for. Hijacking was what it was. An armored car, carrying a factory payroll from a bank. He knew everything about it. Everything. You can't shoot out the tires on one of those armored cars—the guards would just stand inside and call the police on their telephone. Roadblocks are no good either. What you have to do, he said, is hit them while they make a transfer. While the door is open.

He said they were experts. They did dozens of these, all around the country. It was the only way to get the money they needed.

♣

Me and Murray were watching TV. They just arrested this guy in Milwaukee. They found all kinds of bodies in his house. The announcer was saying the guy was maybe the worst serial killer ever. The fire man came in. He listened for a minute, getting excited.

"How many women did he kill?" he asked Murray.

"He only killed boys," Murray said.

"He's a sick bastard," the fire man said, getting up and walking away.

♣

One day, Murray asked me if I wanted to go work out with him. There's a weight room in one of the buildings. I told him no.

"John, come on, man. You're too skinny. I mean, I'm not coming down on you or anything, but I can see you got good musculature . . . a good skeleton, see? If you was to work out with me, I guarantee you, maybe six months, you wouldn't recognize yourself."

"Thanks anyway," I said to him.

He sat down next to me. "John, if I made you feel bad, I'm an asshole. That wasn't what I meant. This whole thing . . ." He waved his arms around. "This whole thing, it's not just for race pride, you know what I mean? Like . . . why did you join up? How come?"

"I hate niggers," I told him.

"Yeah, I know. Me too. As much as anybody. But . . . part of it, I guess . . . I wanted to have friends, too. Real friends. You understand me?"

"Sure."

"So forget about the iron work, okay? I just wanted to say, you got anything I could help you with, you just gotta ask me, okay?"

"Okay, Murray."

He punched me hard on the arm, but I could tell he wasn't trying to hurt me.

♣

The guy in the shoulder holster came by one afternoon. He said the leader wanted to see me.

I followed him over. The leader was in his big room, in his chair. The guy in the shoulder holster left us alone. I measured the distance. I saw the dots start to pop out on him. The door opened behind me—the guy in the white shirt came in.

"You are the young man who knew how to tell a transvestite from a real woman, aren't you?"

"Yes," I said.

"You know why that's so important?"

"No. I don't, I guess."

"The homo-sex-ual doesn't think with his mind, son. He thinks with his sex . . . whatever that is. They're bad apples. One of our great leaders once said, a man who won't fuck won't fight. That's why they don't let them in the army. Just one of them . . . a single one, he can destroy a whole movement. You know, the white power movement didn't start last week. It has a long, honorable history, ever since Reconstruction. . . . You know what that is?"

"No sir."

"After the Civil War, the niggers, the same ones who used to be slaves, they took over the South. Took it over. They were in charge. They owned the land, they owned the women. Naturally, white men could not tolerate this. That was the start of the Klan. And we've been moving forward ever since. Yes, there have been setbacks. But our real enemies have never been the niggers. Our real enemies have always been traitors. Traitors from within. We've got our list, and there's more whites on it than blacks, I can tell you. Judges, senators, FBI agents. All traitors to the race.

"That's why those homo-sex-uals are so dangerous, son. Did you know that one of the real heroes of our movement was actually assassinated by one of his own men? Now that would be hard to explain except for one thing . . . it was a damn lovers' quarrel! You understand? One fag jilted another fag, and we had a shooting. Now, the public doesn't know this, but it's a fact. The worst thing about a fag is how he thinks. So a queer can never be truly white, because he could fall in love with a nigger just like that!"

His fingers made a bone-crack sound when he snapped them. I looked close at him, like he wanted me to.

"You know why I'm telling you all this?"

"No. But it's good to know."

He looked over at the guy in the white shirt. Then he turned back to me.

"You pretty good friends with Murray?"

"I guess."

"He ever . . . act funny around you?"

"No. I never saw him do that."

"You know what I'm getting at?"

"Sure. I seen them before."

"In prison?"

"Yes."

"In prison, you ever see a man with big, huge muscles, tattoos . . . and he's still a queer?"

"Sure," I told him. It was the truth.

"Keep your eyes open," the leader said.

After that, we had meetings every day. Like classes, with teachers. They had this big table, so big we could all fit around it. On the table they had little model cars, roads, and everything. Even a little armored car. They had maps. Not like maps you get in a gas station, black and white maps so big you could see the streets on them.

Some days, the man in the white shirt told us how to do it. Other days, the leader told us why.

They went over it again and again. Every time, they would ask a different guy the same questions. The man in the white shirt pointed at Murray. "What's the procedure if you're captured?"

"I just say I want a lawyer. I don't answer any questions. I just say I want a lawyer."

"Good! One of our lawyers will get to you eventually. Just remember, you may get some Jew Public Defender or something until we can get to you. Don't speak to him either, understand? Wait for the word to get to you."

He looked around the room some more. "Billy, you've got the cash in the getaway car, okay? But when you approach the drop-off point, you see it's covered. What do you do?"

"I find someplace to hole up. I get off the road as soon as I can. Then I call the number and do whatever they tell me to do."

"Right! Now, what if you got a clear shot to make it back here with the money . . . ?"

"We never come back here. Never."

"Why?" the man said, turning his face so he was asking me.

"So the cops don't have an excuse to come in here," I said. I knew all the answers by then, from listening.

"Yes! This is sacred ground. We are all safe here. This is *private property* . . . remember how we talked about that? No cop, no FBI agent, no Treasury man, nobody from ATF . . . *nobody* comes in here without our permission. It's like John here said . . . we can't give them an excuse."

After the meeting, Murray slapped my hand, like he was proud of me for getting it right.

♣

I was watching a nature show on TV. It was quiet in the dorm. They showed different insects that looked like they were dangerous, but they weren't. It was so other animals would leave them alone.

Murray came in. He took off the little weights he wears around his ankles. He wears them around his wrists too. He came over to where I was. The show was just going off.

"How old are you, John?"

"Thirty-four," I told him. Sticking as close as I could

to the truth, like they had told me. The truth is I don't know.

"I'm twenty-nine."

I didn't say anything.

"You were in prison, right?"

"Yeah, I was."

"More than once?"

"Yes."

"I was never in prison. Never in the army either. Or an ex-cop, like some of the guys."

I lit a cigarette. A show about some kind of dancing was coming on.

"You think it matters?" he said.

"What?"

"What I was *saying*, John? Not being in the joint, or the service . . . you know . . ."

"No."

"You know, John, I don't mean to hurt your feelings or nothing, but some of the guys, they think you're not too bright. But me, I know better. You're just quiet is all. I know you got a brain, that's why I ask you stuff."

On the TV, people in white costumes were jumping around. Sometimes the men would catch the women in the air.

"I never forget what you did, John. What you didn't say, I mean. About the stuff in the trailer. We're partners, you and me. Anybody fucks with you, they fuck with me."

He stuck out his hand. I shook it.

♣

There was a lot of training in the place. Everybody was always being trained for something. The men, anyway.

There were women around, but I never saw them being trained.

They practiced so much with the guns. Sometimes the noise was like a wave, it just kept coming.

The Action Team was different. It was quiet. "They look at us different," Murray said to me one time. "Because they know we're on the team." He meant some of the other guys. They looked at us all right—I saw that myself. But I didn't think Murray got it.

In the dorm, it was pretty much okay. There's a bigger place over a few houses down. Like a tavern, I guess. They serve liquor, any kind you want. No charge. And they have a big-screen TV, pool tables, even waitresses. With their clothes on. It's open all the time, I think, but people mostly go there only late in the day.

Murray was always after me to go there. Most of the time I said no. One time I went with him. Some of the guys from another part of the camp were watching us. I always know when someone's watching.

Murray was wearing a black T-shirt, real tight, with the sleeves cut up high. It was a mistake, but I didn't know how to tell him.

I thought they'd start with him, but it was me. One of them banged a shoulder into me as I was carrying a couple of beers over to our table. The beer slopped over and some of it got on him. The guy who pushed me had long hair. A tall man, with fat, loose arms. He told me to watch where the fuck I was going, jabbed me hard in the chest with three fingers held together. I backed up. He came after me, shoving those three fingers at me, calling me names. Murray walked over, moving fast, tapped the guy on the shoulder. The man stepped away from me, three of his friends got up.

"You want to play?" Murray asked the man.

"I don't play with faggots," the man with the fat arms said. His friends laughed. Murray hooked him deep in the stomach. He didn't know how to put his weight behind it —the whole punch was with his arm, but it was enough. The man went down to one knee, trying to breathe.

Two of the man's friends started toward Murray. I cocked the pistol in my hand. It made a loud noise, because everyone was listening. They all stopped.

"Just them," I said.

"Come on, tough guy," Murray said to the man on his knees.

The man didn't get up.

♣

"He's a homo-sex-ual," the leader said.

"A fucking queer," the guy with the shoulder holster said.

"He's on an Action Team. He knows the plans," the guy in the white shirt said.

"It's up to you, son," the leader told me. Then he walked out of the room.

♣

"He has to go," the white shirt said.

"You down to do it?" the shoulder holster asked me.

I looked at him like I was stupid. But it only made things slower, it didn't stop them.

"It's for the cause, John. For the Nation. This Murray, he's dangerous. Probably a government agent."

"A government agent wouldn't kill a nigger," I told him. The acid test, like the crazy man said.

The white shirt looked at the shoulder holster. He put his hand on my shoulder. "Maybe you're right, John. But it doesn't matter. Queers are unreliable. Like the leader taught us. They can't be trusted. Murray . . . that's a Jewish name too, I think. He's gotta go, it's already decided. I know the leader would personally appreciate it if you took care of it."

"All right," I said.

"It's part of the price we pay, John. To be warriors of the white race. It's not his fault he's a queer, but that doesn't matter . . . he's a danger to us all."

They gave me the same gun I had taken with me to the trailers. It was just killing. I felt like I didn't want to do it. I never felt like that before. I thought of Shella. How long I'd been there already. The leader.

If I told them I didn't want to kill Murray, I'd never get close to him alone.

♣

I walked in the dorm. Murray was lying on the bed. He had his shirt off. His hands were locked behind his head. When he does that, the muscles bulge in his arms and his chest. I walked over to him. He smiled. I raised the gun and pulled the trigger. I shot him in the chest three times. Then I shot him twice in the face.

I heard people running out of the dorm.

I sat down in the chair next to my bunk.

♣

The guy in the shoulder holster came in, two other men with him. He took the pistol out of my hand. Gave me a cigarette.

He was talking to me. I wasn't sure what he was saying. I heard one of the other guys whisper, "Just walked in and fucking blasted him right there. . . ."

They rolled Murray's body up in the blankets he was lying on and they carried him out. They took his bunk out too. One of them dumped Clorox on the floor and mopped it around. It made my eyes sting.

The shoulder holster walked over to me. "You did great," he said. "The leader said you were the right man, and he's never wrong about people."

♣

I went for a walk. Nobody said anything to me. In the woods, I saw a butterfly. A big one, black with little spots of yellow and blue. When I was a kid, in one of those places they kept me, I saw a butterfly come out, get born from a shell. I remembered it then, when I was walking. What I saw. It was brand new, wet. It flapped its wings to dry them off. I was watching it happen. One of the bigger boys came up. He was mean and nasty, asked me why I was crying. I didn't know I was, until he said it. He grabbed the butterfly before it could fly away and he crushed it in his fist. He thought it was funny.

They taught me not to cry in there.

♣

The next day, they took me to see the leader. This time, they searched me. Real close. Not as much as they did the first time, but they still touched me everywhere.

"You're gonna be alone with him," the shoulder holster said.

They opened the door and we walked in. The leader got up from behind his desk. He came over to me, stuck out his hand for me to shake. He looked over at the shoulder holster. They kind of nodded to each other and the shoulder holster walked out. He closed the door behind him.

I was alone with the leader.

He sat down behind his desk, pointed me to a chair.

"You are a true warrior of the right, John," he told me. "Sometimes it's hard to do what is necessary . . . a man shows his true color under fire. You showed white. You showed right. On behalf of our people, I appreciate what you did."

"Thanks."

"You're going to be spending some time with me every day from now on, learning some things. How's that sound to you?"

"Good." Black dots jumped out on his face. Faint dots. I watched his mouth move while he talked, waiting for the dots to get darker. The door opened. The man with the shoulder holster came in.

"There's a call," he said to the leader.

The leader stood up. He made a sort of salute at me. I walked out. They both stayed in the room.

♣

I went over there every day. They always searched me.
Nobody was allowed to be near the leader with a weapon,
they said.

One day, the leader got up, made a motion like I was to
come along. We walked all around the compound. He was
talking to me. About the race. Loyalty. A true white man.
The shoulder holster was always close.

Near the back of the compound, there was a whole lot
of men standing around.

"Here's a treat," the leader said. "Come on, John."

Men were standing around a ring. I thought it was going
to be fighters until we got close. They stood aside so the
leader could step up. I was right next to him.

The ring was maybe fifteen feet across. A wood wall went
all around it. It came to just past my knee. The floor was
canvas. There was lines drawn on it.

"You ever see one of these before?" the leader asked me.
I saw the dogs then. "No," I told him.

He looked at his watch. "Roscoe's the next match?" he
asked the shoulder holster.

The other guy nodded.

It was quiet for a minute. Then men climbed into the
ring, carrying dogs in their arms. The one closest to us was
a big black dog with a white patch on his chest. The guy
holding him said something to the leader—I couldn't catch
what it was.

"That's him!" the leader said.

The other dog was white, with a black patch over one
eye. One ear was black too. He was smaller than the black

one. The guys with the dogs were rubbing them. One put his dog in a tub and gave him a bath. Money was flying all around, people betting.

A man climbed in the ring, stood in the middle. He pointed at each of the men with dogs. They both nodded. Picked up their dogs and carried them forward. There was a line in the center. The referee stood on it. Each man came up to another line. They put their dogs down, held them between their legs, facing each other. The dogs were crazy to charge.

"Go!" the referee said, and both dogs ran together.

They fought hard, ripping. They locked together a couple of times, and the referee used a stick to break them apart.

People were screaming. "He can't be beat!" the leader yelled, right in my ear.

Sometimes they would take the dogs into their corners. The men holding them would face them away from the center, looking at the wall, so they wouldn't get crazy. They then would pick them up and bring them back to the center. When the referee said "Go!" they let the dogs free.

They fought a long time. The white dog's muzzle was all ripped, one of the black dog's eyes was gone, somewhere on the floor. When they brought them back, the white dog couldn't stand up.

"Go!"

The white dog crawled toward the black dog, ready to die. The black dog leaped on him. The white dog rolled on his back and nailed the black dog in the neck. Blood was all around his muzzle, but he couldn't keep the hold.

I figured it out. Every time they broke the dogs, it was a different dog's turn to move forward first. If they didn't go forward, they lost. If they did, one had to die.

The black dog won every time they hit, but the white dog never quit.

They faced them again, and the white dog crawled forward. He kept crawling. The black dog stood there, watching him. The white dog stopped. People screamed at him. A long time passed. The referee waved his arms.

"He quit!" one guy yelled near the wall. He looked mad.

"He's dead," another one said.

The man was holding his white dog in his arms. I could see he was crying.

The man with the black dog came over to the leader. He held up his bloody dog like a prize.

"Never defeated!" the leader said.

We stayed there. After a while, the other guy came over to the leader, carrying his white dog.

"You should be proud of him," the leader said. "He was dead game."

The guy kissed his dead dog. "You hear that, Razor? You hear that? Dead game, boy! That's you! Dead game!"

He was crying when he walked away.

♣

I was mostly in the dorm by myself, nights. Sometimes I went for a walk, looked at the dark woods. I could never see anything.

I was alone a lot with the leader, days. But I could never get the rhythm, never could tell when someone was coming in.

"You learn anything from the fight?" the leader asked me.

"I don't know."

"Dead game, what that means for pit bulls, it means they never quit. That's the quality you want, gameness. You know why we fight the dogs?"

"To watch them?"

"No, son. I know it must look like that, people screaming, betting, and all that. But the reason is to improve the breed. If you want a dog to be game, you have to test him. Only the true champions get to breed. . . . That way you get rid of the curs, the ones that will quit. You breed only game dogs, you get only game puppies, see?"

"The white dog, it was game?"

"All the way. Not a drop of quit in that beast."

"But it won't breed."

"Well, no. It won't. Only the best, John. Only the very, very best. What you want is pure."

♣

He talked a lot to me about Valhalla. Where warriors go when they die. If they die the right way. It's a perfect place for a man, he said.

He told me about dying. How it can be perfect. A perfect sacrifice for the race.

He said the white pit bull died for love. Love of its master. That's why they fight to the death, he said. For love.

He was talking about race when there was a knock from behind him. I didn't know there was a door there. He didn't act like he heard it. The knocking came again.

Finally, he got up and opened the door that was behind a curtain. A young woman came in. Pregnant, real heavy in front.

"John, this is my daughter, Melissa."

She kind of giggled at me. He talked to her, quiet-voice. She was touching his arm, patting at it. There was a button on his desk. He reached over and pushed it. The door opened behind me and shoulder holster came in. He looked at the leader, said "Come on" to me, put his hand on my arm to take me out of there.

As I was going, the girl looked at me. I saw her eyes and I saw what Shella must've seen.

♣

The more I practiced with the guns, the more they watched me do it. Every time I held a gun in my hand, I would feel it. What it could do.

I could do it too—I just had to be close.

I kept the gun with me all the time. So they'd expect it. Once, I was looking for a place to put it while I took a shower. They give us plenty of room for things here—not like in prison. Some of the guys had foot lockers, some of them had trunks. Most of the guys, they didn't stay in the compound anyway, they just came and went. I was the longest man in the dorm.

I couldn't think of a place to put the gun. I didn't want to leave it on my bunk. There was a row of metal lockers against the far wall. I looked there, but they all had locks on them. Then I saw it—Murray's trunk. I remembered it because it was this dark-red color, with black bands around it. It was all covered with dust, just sitting there in the corner.

Nobody was around. I didn't break the lock, I unscrewed the plate. Shella told me how to do that, once when we were trying to get into someplace.

Inside the trunk Murray had his clothes. And his little
weight things for his wrists and his ankles. There was a
bunch of letters. He had them tied with a ribbon. They
looked old.

He had a jacket in there. It was black, with big white
sleeves. It felt like silk. On the front, over the heart, it said
Ace in little white letters, like writing. On the back it said
the name of some gym.

I put my gun in his trunk while I took my shower. I fixed
the lock plate so I could just pull it off with my fingers
when I came out.

♣

"Who brought him in?" the leader asked the guy in the
white shirt. Like I wasn't there. It didn't make me mad—
people always do that.

The white shirt always has the long flat aluminum box
with him. When he opens it up, there's pads and stuff
inside. He looked there for a minute. "Mack," he told the
leader.

The leader looked at me. "Mack say anything to you about
the Lightning Squadron?"

"Yes."

"What?"

"He said he was a scout."

"Anything else?"

"No."

The leader gave white shirt one of those looks I never
understand—it could mean anything.

♣

Every day was the same after that. Every day I would get up and walk around. Sometimes I would look at the posters. THE JEWS ARE THROUGH IN '92, was one I saw a lot. Then I would take my gun and go over and practice. After that, I'd walk back to the dorm. More people would be out by then. There would be kids too, dressed up like the older people in soldier suits with little guns. Some of them wore armbands . . . red with white circles and the black crooked cross inside . . . and they said nigger and kike and spic and that kind of thing like they were learning their ABCs or something.

They were always beating the kids. With sticks and belts. And slapping them. I saw a man whipping a little boy. The boy was screaming. The man's wife said it was good discipline and everyone standing around nodded. I walked away. When I looked back, the others were watching the little boy get whipped.

I would look at TV until one of them came for me. They would walk over with me. Then they would take my gun and search me so I could go inside with the leader. Sometimes there were other people there, sometimes we were alone. Sometimes his daughter came in. He never talked on the phone they had in his office. When it would ring, somebody else would take it.

I never knew if I would be alone with him. I never knew how long it would last.

Every day, the same talk from him. Master race, masters and slaves, serving the master. The Lightning Squad, it would strike like lightning at the enemies of the race. Some of the members, they wouldn't get out. But they would go to Valhalla for sure. Guaranteed.

Nobody ever talked so much to me. Nobody ever explained things like he did, except maybe Shella.

On one wall of his office, he had pictures. Pictures of men. Each one was in a metal frame. He said those men gave their lives for the Nation. They were heroes. Heroes of the race. The children who went to their schools would memorize their names.

He said the niggers weren't human, so you couldn't really blame them for the animal way they acted. The Jews, you could blame them. They knew what they were doing. They were a different race, even though they looked like us. You could tell the difference, but only if you knew them real good.

The leader told me that we were going to win, because we were superior. And because the niggers were starting to really hate the Jews and the Jews were going to have to do something about it.

He gave me books to read. One was a little red book, some kind of story. One of them said PROTOCOLS on it. I tried to read it. I'm not stupid. But I couldn't understand it. When he asked me, I told him the truth.

He said that was okay—the important thing was, would I do the right thing when the time came?

I always said I would.

Once in a while, they would ask me if I wanted a woman. I always said I did.

When I was fucking one of the women, I wondered if they had ever asked Murray if he wanted one.

♣

Every day, it got dark quicker at the end. It started to get colder. I didn't have a jacket with me, just what was in my duffel bag. When they searched me one day, before I went inside to be alone with the leader, they said why wasn't I wearing a jacket. I told them it wasn't that cold yet.

They must have a way the men outside could talk to the leader, because he asked me if I had a jacket. He said, if I didn't, I could grab a ride into town with Rex and pick one up. I didn't know who Rex was, but I figured out he meant the guy with the shoulder holster.

I never found out the name of the guy with the white shirt and the clipboard.

I told the leader I already had a jacket. He said I should start wearing it, otherwise I could catch a cold.

♣

The next morning, I remembered what the leader said before they came over to get me. I went into Murray's locker and got his black-and-white jacket. It was way too big for me when I put it on.

The men who searched me hadn't seen the jacket before. They made me take it off. They went through it real careful, but there was nothing in it.

They kept my gun. I carried the jacket inside with me to be with the leader.

It was never going to get any better. I knew that. It wasn't that I couldn't wait—I can always wait. But it would never change, I could see that.

He was talking and talking. I moved around a little bit,

listening to him, always watching his face. He kicked back in his chair, put his feet on the desk. I never saw him do that before. I guessed there was a button he could push, bring the other men inside. There's always a button like that in back rooms. He put his hands behind his head, the way Murray used to do. But there was no muscles bulging.

The way his hands and his feet were, he couldn't push a button real fast.

I got up, started to walk around a bit. I did that before. It didn't make him nervous anymore.

When his head tilted back, I saw the black dots pop out on his Adam's apple. The place where you can tell the real men.

I walked just past his feet, so close I could smell him. My back was to him for a second. I planted my foot and spun around. His mouth came open. I hit him so hard in the throat he couldn't make a sound even if he was alive. I pushed his face against the desk and held him there while I broke his neck from behind.

I didn't have a plan to get out. I started choking him. He let go while I was still squeezing—I could smell it.

His daughter walked in. Just walked in, didn't make a sound. She had a denim shift on, barefoot, a red scarf around her neck. Her belly was really big. She looked at me. I saw the blue marks high on her arms, where someone had grabbed her hard. I moved to her before she could get out the way she came in, but she just stood there.

She didn't say anything. Then she moved her hand, just a little bit. I stepped next to her, put my hand on the back of her neck. I gave it a little squeeze. Not to hurt her, just to tell her.

When I took my hand away, she didn't move.

I picked up Murray's jacket and put it on, watching her.

Something told me, told me so I knew. If she screamed, it wouldn't matter. Even if she screamed, the guards wouldn't come in.

She turned around, away from me. Started moving out the way she came in. I was right behind her. It was a whole apartment in one big room. A kitchen against one wall. The ceiling was very high. There was a platform on the wall, with chains holding it, like a bed in an old jail. A ladder so you could climb up there, maybe to sleep. I could tell it was just for her—the leader didn't live there.

I pushed her to a chair. She sat down without me having to do anything to her.

I looked out the window. It wasn't far to the woods. I stayed close to her. The red scarf around her neck, I took it off her, tied it around my head.

I couldn't take her out the window—she'd never make it up and through. I looked for something to tie her up with. She stood up quick, opened a door. There was a platform there, a little platform with steps to the ground. I saw a man with a baseball cap turn around when he heard the door open. I never saw him before. He had a machine gun on a sling over his shoulder.

"Come on," the girl said, and started down the stairs.

I came right behind her. I had to get close to the man with the gun. He started coming toward us, but his hands were away from the gun. I had my hand just behind her, on her waist. Soon as he came near enough . . .

The woods were close. Real close.

The man stopped. Too far away. "What's going on?" he said.

"He's just taking me into town. In the truck. To buy some things," she said.

"The leader didn't say anything to me about that."

"So what? You think I need his permission just to go into town?"

"Yeah, you do," a man's voice said. A voice from behind us.

I knew it then—I'd never see Shella.

♣

"Get your hands up, boy! Fast!"

I raised my hands.

"Step away from her . . . move!"

I did that too. The man who'd been behind us stood to one side. He had a pistol, a big chrome one. Aimed right at me. The guy in the baseball cap, he had both hands on his gun too.

"He told me to watch out for you," the guy with the pistol said. I could tell, the way he said it, he meant the girl.

"Let's take them both back," the man with the machine gun said. "Let the leader decide. You . . . let's go," pointing at me with his chin.

It didn't matter, but the woods were so close I had to try. I stumbled a little so I could get next to him, but the guy stepped back and then I heard something like a real quiet motorcycle trying to start and both of them went down, blood and bone flying from their heads.

I ran for the woods.

♣

I got over the fence in a flash. When I dropped down on the other side, there was nobody there. I ran away from the fence, hard as I could.

The Indian was there. Just standing there. I couldn't see where he came from. He had a rifle in his hand, a long rifle with a tube over the barrel. He moved his hand, like in a wave, and I followed him.

There was a Jeep at the end of the trail we went down. A black Jeep. I got in the back with the Indian—there was two men in the front seat already. We took off.

The Indian picked up a phone, touched one button.

"We're off," he said. "It's still quiet here. Check with the post, get back to me."

The driver was going through the woods like it was a street.

The phone made a noise. The Indian picked it up. "Go," he said. Then he listened.

"They found the bodies," he said to the men in the front seat. "They can't get a ring up in time. Sam's team will give 'em something else to think about in a minute, but we gotta go through the roadblock on our own."

The man in the passenger seat reached up over the windshield. He pulled something down, like a window shade. Only you could see it was metal. There was a thin slit in it. The driver leaned forward, looking through it. There was shades like that for the windows too, even the back window. I pulled mine down.

The Indian opened this case he had on the floor. I saw grenades, one of those little machine guns, some other stuff. It made metal clicking sounds when the Indian snapped it all together.

"Get on the floor," he told me. I did that and then there was this explosion. Like a bomb. From somewhere behind us.

"One more corner," the man in the passenger seat said.

The Indian slid up his metal window shade and poked a gun out the open window.

I felt the Jeep slide around a long corner and then it was nothing but blasting. Bullets smacked into the Jeep but all I could hear was the guns. The Jeep kept moving. I felt it hit something, then we were through.

The Jeep came to a stop.

"Come on!" the Indian told me.

We got out. The Jeep was smoking, one tire was off. There were two cars at the roadblock and a lot of dead people.

♣

We got into the woods again. The man who'd been in the passenger seat went first. Then the driver, then me, then the Indian.

We stopped after a bit. The driver was bleeding down one side of his face. He didn't seem like he knew it. The Indian took a little box out of his pocket. He pushed a button on it and there was a booming sound. We started off again. Then there was a loud sound like a firebomb.

"Gas tank," the Indian said to me. He took the phone out of the holster, pushed a button. "Six," is all he said. Then he listened.

The others looked at him.

"They're there," the Indian said. Then he took the lead and we followed him.

♣

Near the edge of the woods there was a big gray Ford. Me and the Indian got in the back seat. I saw the other two guys get in another car, a brown Chevy. There was another Jeep there too, a white one.

When we came onto the paved road, the white Jeep was in front and we followed.

The Indian lit a cigarette, offered me one.

"Nice jacket," he said.

I touched Murray's jacket with my fingers.

"They'll remember it," the Indian said. "We should of left it there."

I didn't say anything.

He waited, smoking his cigarette.

I leaned forward in the seat, took off Murray's jacket, and handed it to him.

"We'll hold it for you," he said.

♣

They didn't say much, but you could feel how tight they were. When the Indian moved in the seat next to me, I could see the little sparks all around him. I thought we'd go to their camp, but we drove all the way back to Chicago, straight on through. The car stopped in front of the apartment house where I stayed before.

When we got upstairs, it looked the same.

"I'll be back tonight," the Indian told me. "I'll tell you everything then."

♣

I took a shower, changed my clothes. There was food in the refrigerator. I listened to the radio, but there was nothing about what happened in Indiana. Maybe they bury their own dead.

I knew the Indian would come back. Otherwise, they would have just left me after I did the job. Left me right in that compound.

I wondered why they didn't. Maybe Indians don't do that.

After a while, I found a nature show on TV.

♣

I heard the Indian let himself in but I didn't move. The only light was the TV screen, but he came through the apartment like he could see.

He sat down across from me. "You did it perfect," he said. "Glided in right under their radar."

"Where is she?" I asked him.

He took some paper out of his pocket. Handed it to me. It was pages from a magazine, black and white. One page was folded back at the corner. A woman was standing there. In the light from the TV, I could see she had high black boots, something in her hand. There was another woman next to her, kneeling on a couch or something.

I turned on the light. The woman standing was blonde. Her hair was long. Her arms and shoulders were heavy. Big. Almost like Murray's. The woman kneeling next to her had a dog collar around her neck. She was stripped naked. The big woman was holding a leash in one hand.

A little whip with a lot of strings on it in the other.
It wasn't a real good picture, but I could see enough.

"That's her?" the Indian asked.

I told him it was.

♣

Later he showed me a lot of other stuff. Mostly pictures.
Shella with a girl over her knee, like she was spanking
her. Shella whipping a man, his hands tied way above his
head. Shella with her hands on her hips, like she was giving
orders. He showed me some ads too. Mistress Katrina.
Discipline lessons, private. In one picture, Shella had a
girl all tied up, clothespins clamped on the tips of her
breasts, a gag in her mouth. It was all Shella, even if she
looked different every picture.

"We don't have any close-ups," the Indian said. "The
crazy man said all this stuff was old, at least a couple a
years, okay? But if that's her, we know where she is now."

"Where?"

"We'll take you to her," he said.

♣

The next morning, he was back. "It'll take a couple a days
to set it up, all right? We got a long way to travel, we have
to make all the arrangements."

He had more papers with him. A police sheet with arrests
on it, all different names. Girls' names. He said that was
Shella too.

"I wasn't there every day," he said after a while.

"Where?"

"In the woods. We figured it out, finally. Where you were going every day. It had to be his house. But he didn't live there. He went in the same door you did. The front door. Every day. There's no angle on it, even from the woods, it's shielded by the other buildings, like in a tunnel. No way to get a shot off. The back, that was easy, but he never went there. The woman, the pregnant one? She would go outside sometimes, but she never got far."

"Did she . . . ?"

"We didn't shoot her. She didn't scream either."

I didn't say anything. After a while, he started talking again.

"When we saw you come out with the bandanna on your head, we knew it was done. If you'd gone out the front, you wouldn't have made it. No way we could cover you. And we couldn't get a message in. All we could do is wait."

"It's okay."

"He's dead. I guess you know that. There wasn't nothing in the papers, but the crazy man, he found out. He said he's satisfied. That's when he turned over the information . . . about your woman."

"We're going soon?"

"Day after tomorrow."

♣

The next day, he gave me an envelope full of money. "We sold your Chevy," he said. "Everything else too. It's all gone. You're starting over. This is all new ID, like he promised. You can buy whatever you need when you decide."

"Decide what?"

He just shrugged, like I knew what he was talking about.

♣

Three of them came up the morning we left. The Indian stepped to one side. "This is Joseph. This is Amos," he said. They held out their hands and we shook. I knew them—they were in the front seat of the Jeep when we came through the roadblock. Amos was the driver.

"They're volunteers," the Indian said.

Downstairs, we got in another Jeep. A red one. They really liked Jeeps, the Indians. They had all kinds of stuff piled in, even stuff on the roof.

"Hunting trip," the Indian said to me.

We took off.

"Better to stay off planes," the Indian said. "I don't think they know anything, but they might have a picture or something. They won't look for long—they're not professionals. For now, this is better."

We just kept driving, like Amos never got tired. The Indian talked. Sometimes Amos talked. Joseph, he just watched.

By the time they decided to stop, we were someplace in Nebraska.

♣

Amos and Joseph took one room in the motel. I guess they always stayed together. The Indian and me had a room too.

"We got about another day's drive," he told me. "Five, six hundred miles. We'll leave first light, time it so we get there next morning coming."

"Okay."

It was quiet in the room. The Indian told me about his tribe. I listened with my eyes closed. When he stopped speaking, I opened my eyes.

"The crazy man kept his word?" I asked him.

"Sure. We're just taking you to her ourselves to finish —not because we don't believe him."

"But you want to see for yourselves?"

He looked across at me, nodded his head.

"What about the rest?"

"The rest?"

"Hiram. Ruth's brother. Did they transfer him?"

The Indian didn't say anything. He looked at me for a long time. Then he dropped his eyes, played with a cigarette until he got it going.

"You remembered his name . . . ?"

I was surprised too. I didn't know I even knew his name until I said it out loud like that.

The Indian got up, walked around a little bit. I closed my eyes again. I felt him come close to me, sit down on the bed near my chair.

"Hiram was transferred the next day. They must have been typing the papers the minute the body hit the ground. They moved him into a Level Three joint. Cake. We can go in and get him anytime we want. It'll take a while, set it up properly. But our brother has spent his last winter behind the walls."

"Then . . ."

"He wouldn't cheat us, John. It wouldn't be worth it to him. But he might not know how things are. . . . You're with us, understand?"

"With you?"

"Until it's done. You did your piece. You did it perfect.

We think she's there. But we're not walking in the front door waving a sign. She's there, it's done. Like we agreed. She's not there . . ."

"What?"

"We'll find her. All of us."

♣

Amos kept the Jeep near other cars all the time, always rolling in the middle. He'd move from pack to pack, so smooth you could hardly feel it. He held the wheel loose in his hands, just flicked it a little bit when he wanted to move. Every couple of hours, he would move the seat. Forward, back. Up, down. Every time he did that, he would move the mirrors too.

I saw the overhead signs—we were in Arizona. Joseph turned around in the seat.

"No more problems, brother. Plenty of places to disappear to now."

The Indian looked at him. "They'd rat us out just as fast on the damn reservations. We only have ourselves."

Joseph nodded, turned around to look out his window.

We found a motel. Amos dropped us off, went away to get some stuff for the car.

"She's close," the Indian told me. "We go in tomorrow, soon as it opens up."

"What?"

"A hospital," he said, looking at me. "A hospital in the desert."

♣

The Indian was on his bed, smoking with the lights out. It was late, past midnight. I could see the red tip of his cigarette.

"Wolf?"

"What?"

"You think she's there?"

He smoked the whole cigarette through, ground it out in the ashtray. After a long time, he said "Yes."

SHELLA

In the morning, I felt like I should do something different, but I couldn't think of what it should be. It was still dark. The Indian wasn't in his bed.

He walked in about an hour later.

"You want some breakfast before we go? Some coffee?"

"I'm okay."

"What're you doing?" he asked me, looking at the bed where I had my stuff laid out.

"Packing."

He nodded his head, walked out again.

By the time he came back, I was ready to go. But when I put the duffel bag over my shoulder, the Indian shook his head.

"What?" He was looking at the room key in my hand.

"We're not going by the front desk. It's paid for a few days, but if things don't work out, we're gonna keep rolling. . . . You don't check out, they'll think you're coming back."

"Who would?"

He just shrugged his shoulders . . . not like he didn't know, like it didn't matter.

♠

Amos pulled the Jeep over to the side of the road on a long curve. I could see a bunch of white buildings on the right.

"Stay with Amos for a little bit," the Indian said. "We'll be back soon."

I saw the flash of a shoulder holster on Joseph as he climbed out the front seat. I guessed the Indian had one with him too. They started walking away.

Amos drove off, with me in the back seat. "It's all right," he told me. "We checked it last night, top to bottom. Just wanted to be sure, one more time."

He circled around, a long loop. No matter where he drove, I could always see the white buildings.

It took about half an hour. Then Amos pulled to a bus stop. The Indian and Joseph were sitting on a bench, like they'd been there for days. They climbed back in the Jeep.

In the parking lot, the Indian took a bunch of papers out of his coat. He smoothed them on his lap, pointed out a name to me. Olivia Oltraggio.

"That's the name she's using," he said.

I looked at it deep. Said it to myself over and over, so I'd know it. I couldn't say the last name. The Indian said it for me. Slow. In four parts. It sounded Italian. She had been there almost three months . . . I could see that from the papers. It said Ward Four. The Indian turned over the papers, tapped his finger again. She was in Room 303, starting a few days ago.

"It's a private room," the Indian said. "They had her moved once it was done."

I reached for my duffel. Felt the Indian's hand on my arm. "Leave it here," he said. "Outside her room, right next to it, there's a staircase. You have to get out of there fast, go down the staircase. *All* the way down, to the basement. Turn to your left, go past the laundry room, there's a fire door there, a red door. You know the kind . . . you push the handle and the alarm goes off . . . emergency exit? You push it, nothing's gonna happen, no noise, but the . door'll open, okay? We'll be outside, keep you covered."

"I'll be—"

"Right to the end," the Indian said. "You come out the front door, there's no problem, just get into the Jeep, drive it away yourself. Here's the keys. Your stuff'll be in the back. Go back to the motel, go someplace else, it's up to you."

I heard a door open. Joseph was already out, moving to the front of the building.

"When you get inside, just get on the elevator, the one right past the front desk. Go on up to the room, understand?"

"Yes."

The Indian nodded at me, and I got out too. When I walked in the front door, I couldn't see Joseph.

♠

I went over to the elevator. Thinking it's good that people never pay attention to me. There were people in white coats on the elevator, talking. I stood to the side. Got off on the third floor.

There was a sign there with an arrow. I walked down the corridor. People were going in and out of the rooms. It smelled like a prison with flowers.

The stairway was at the end. Room 303 right next to it.

There was one of those thin holders on the door, where they slide a piece of plastic in it with a person's name. To tell you who's inside. The name she was using was there. White letters on the blue plastic. It looked strange.

The door was closed. I pushed it open—it made a little hiss. The back wall was all glass. A bed was there, parallel to it. The sun slanted in—it was hard to see. The door closed by itself behind me. I stepped over to the bed and a face turned to me. It was all eyes, shrunken.

"I knew you'd come," Shella said.

♠

My legs locked. I moved toward her. . . . I felt like the white pit bull, crawling to the line. There was a brick in my chest. Right in the center of my chest, not over my heart.

I got there. Her hair was long, more white than blonde now, like dead straw, thin. Everything about her was thin, her arms were sticks. As she turned, the nightgown fell away. . . . her breasts were almost gone. Her cheeks were sucked in, big splotches on her face, dark ones. . . . I couldn't see the beauty mark I made for her.

I saw her teeth. I couldn't tell if she was smiling or snarling. She held out her hand.

I moved closer. I could hear a crackling in my chest, like when you crush the stuff they put around cigarette packs in your hand. I got close enough to touch her. She looked up at me.

"Hello, John," she said, real quiet. "If you came to kill me, you're too late."

♠

I just stood and looked at her. Shella. It was Shella.

"Same old motormouth, aren't you?" she said. She shifted her hips under the sheet, patted the bed for me to sit down.

I did that. She put her hand on my thigh, the way she used to, like it was hers. The sun came in on her hand. I could see every bone in it.

I closed my eyes. Breathed as slow as I could. I could feel her doing it too.

When I opened my eyes, hers were still closed, but she wasn't asleep.

"What happened?" I asked her.

♠

She didn't say anything for a long time. I didn't move. "You don't look any different," she said. "I knew you wouldn't. You're not gonna die slow."

"What happened, Shella? Why did you go?"

"Ah, who knows?" she said. "I got a whore's heart. Maybe I just got bored. What does it matter anyway?"

"I've been looking for you . . . for a long time."

"Why?"

"For you to tell me the truth."

She opened her eyes. "The truth-truth? The real thing?"

"Yes."

"I was afraid of you."

"Of me? Of me, Shella? I never did . . ."

"I know. When I took off, in the car, with everything

. . . I didn't go far. I drove for about an hour, and I got a room. The next day, I got out of the motel and I rented a furnished apartment. A nice studio. There was nothing in the papers until the next day. I could see it was gonna be a while before you went to trial. I figured I'd get work, wiggle my big butt enough to make some money, get you a good lawyer. I knew you wouldn't want me to come and visit in the jail. . . . They might be waiting on me . . . know you had a partner."

"A partner . . . sure, that's right."

"Yeah. Anyway, I started working. The next thing I knew, you were gone. I found out you pleaded guilty. After they took you down . . . oh Jesus, John . . . you expected me to be there, didn't you? Waiting for you when you stepped out of the gate."

"I thought you would stay," I told her.

"I *couldn't* stay, you fucking moron! What was I gonna do? Buy a house, get a job at McDonald's . . . what?"

"I don't . . ."

"People like us, we can't stay in one place. It's bad rhythm, dumb. You know *that* much, right?"

"I guess. . . ."

"I was never that far away. Not in my mind. I called the PD, told him I was your sister. He ran it down for me. I knew how much time you had to serve. . . . I went out on the track, got lost in the scene for a while."

I must of looked stupid at her when she said that—she kind of shifted gears with her voice. "You remember Bonnie? That skinny bitch I owned back when we had that beach cottage?"

I nodded.

"Like that," she said. "Most of them, just like that. I did some men too, but not many."

I looked around the room. It was a nice room. Big and clean. There was a TV set on the end of a metal arm, a stand-up shower over to the side. Behind the bed I could see a pair of tanks, like for propane gas. I took out a cigarette.

"Go ahead," Shella said. "It doesn't make any difference."

I lit the smoke. "Give me some," she said, the way she used to, moving against me. I handed her the smoke. She took a deep drag, handed it back. She was watching me close. She kept watching until I took a drag myself, then she lay back and closed her eyes again.

I thought maybe she was tired, but she started to talk again.

"By the time I came up for air, they had cut you loose. I took a plane, I was in such a hurry. I didn't think it would be so bad, so hard finding you. Some man would know where you were, on parole. I could always make men tell me things. I got a room in a real nice hotel. I had a whole bunch of money too, John. Your share. I kept your share for you, all the time. I was all excited. Like maybe the other stuff was over, I don't know."

"I—"

"Shut up. Talking makes me tired. Let me finish this piece. I called the parole office. When I asked for your PO, they made me wait a long time. That's the way they do, anyway. . . . It didn't spook me. But when the man came on the line, he wouldn't give me your address. Not over the phone, he said. I'd have to come in. I knew it then. I put down the phone. It only took me a couple of nights to find the right guy. A guy on parole. I promised him some pussy and he came back to the same joint in a couple of days, after he reported in himself. He told me you hung up the parole . . . that you were a fugitive. There was a warrant out for you. . . . When they got you, you'd have to serve the rest of your time. A crazy move, not like you. So I figured you were coming after me. I ran. I kept running. . . ."

"Shella . . ."

"I'm tired now, John. Real tired. I just drift off when I get like this. They're gonna come in with my shots soon anyway. Just let me go, now. Come back in a couple of hours, okay?"

"Sure. I didn't . . ."

"I'm not going anywhere," she said, closing her eyes.

♠

I don't remember walking out of the hospital. I think I took the elevator, but I don't remember. The next thing I knew I was on the bench. The bench where you wait for the bus, where the Indian and Joseph were before. A bus came, but I didn't move. Other people got on, but I didn't. I knew people were looking at me after a while. I knew it was stupid to stay there. I knew I was stupid.

I got up and walked. Around and around. I knew that was stupid too. People would notice me. I couldn't find a dark crowd.

I saw a sign. TOPLESS. Inside, the cold came right at me. It must have been hot outside. It was the same as all the other places. The daytime girls are never the best. They're tired, like they have jobs at night too.

I bought drinks and didn't drink them, like always. They didn't really have acts in that place. The girls came on and danced to records. Men watched. Nobody was laughing. It was quiet watchers, mostly.

All the girls looked alike, but I knew that couldn't be. I guess I wasn't paying attention.

I sat at the bar until time passed around me. There was no clock there, and I didn't have a watch.

After a while, I got up and went back outside.

♠

I went in the hospital like I was going in the first time again. The elevator was there. Everything was the same.

Her door was closed. I pushed it open. She was sitting up in the bed, watching. There was a chair next to her bed. She saw me and moved her hand, like I should sit down. I went over and did it.

"You know what I have?" she asked me.

"I . . . guess."

"Yeah. I'm gone, John. My T-cell count's down below two hundred."

"You have money?"

"Money? It doesn't make any difference now. That's why they moved me to this private room. That's the way they do things here. It bothers the other patients to see someone go out—makes it harder to swallow all the bullshit about a positive mental attitude."

"How . . . ?"

"How *what?* What difference could it make now?"

I didn't say anything for a while. "I did a lot of things," I told her. "I did a lot of things, trying to find you."

"You always did a lot of things, John."

We stayed quiet after that. I smoked a couple of cigarettes, shared them with her. Nobody came in. The sun shifted lower in the sky but it was still coming in her window.

Maybe I fell asleep. I heard her voice like it was in the middle, like she'd been talking for a while.

"I went too far, honey," she said. "I went too far. I hated them so much. I still hate them."

"Who?"

"My father."

"Did you . . . ?"

"No. I never saw him. But I kept seeing him. You understand what I'm saying? I just kept seeing him. I was working as a domina. I never had sex. I never had sex since you went down, John. You believe that?"

"Yes. I was just . . ."

"What?"

"I was . . . confused."

"That's you. Confused. You're always confused, aren't you? I'm surprised you made it this far. People always use you. . . . I thought you'd be used up. All used up. It's funny, huh? I know how things work, you don't. And I'm the one—"

"Shella—"

"I never had sex with any of them. Not real sex. I never made a whore's mistake, either. Whores're stupid. They think because a man will pay them to piss on his face they can laugh at him. I knew a whore got herself killed doing that. You can't laugh unless you've got control. . . . It doesn't matter who's paying."

"It doesn't—"

"Everything matters. Everything gets paid for. My tricks, they could get off being whipped, when I hurt them. Sometimes they'd finish themselves. But I never let anyone inside me. I could have stayed on the phones. There's real money in that. Talking to freaks. Plug in a credit card and close your eyes and you get what you want. But some of them, they wanted the real thing. And they paid more for it. A lot more. It used to help me too. It was enough, for a while. I'd put on my outfit and make them lick my boots, tie them up, blindfold them. It felt . . . powerful. But as soon as it was over, they'd get dressed and they wouldn't look at you. They'd go back to being in charge. They got what they paid for. No matter what you did to them, they were calling the shots. Using you, the way they always do."

I touched her arm. The bones in her arm. "You don't have to do that anymore. . . ."

"I never *had* to do it, John. Remember what the little gangster in New York used to call you? Ghost? That's what I was, a ghost. It wasn't real. Spanking. That's what some of them call it. Spanking. Like the way you'd do a kid. Some of them did it. To kids, I mean. Some of them go both ways. Like AC-DC, but with the whip. Switch, they call it. If you're a switch, you'll give it and you'll take it. I never took it."

"I know."

She acted like she didn't hear me. "I worked the dungeons first, but then went out on my own. They have such a cute name for it. Domestic Discipline. One day, I had one of them tied up. Before we started, he showed me pictures of his little girls. Two little girls. Told me how he spanked them when they were bad. He had pictures of them. With their pants down. He told me maybe he'd bring them over to me. For discipline, he said. He wanted to watch. I was working on him. Saying the words. Like dancing. I saw his face. It was him. My father. Tied up and he couldn't move. I could see his hard-on bulging and I wanted to cut it off."

"It's all right," I told her.

"Shut up! I need to finish this. You came all this way to hear the truth. . . . Sit there and take it. Take it!"

I moved my fingers along her arm, trying to find a vein. Her skin was so pale I could see through it.

"I beat him to death. Halfway through, he got it. Knew I wasn't going to stop. There was a gag in his mouth. A good gag, big rubber ball. I don't know if he choked to death on the vomit or his heart just stopped or what. But I could smell when he died. I ran out of there then. I was scared. Scared of myself. But I went back. Right back to it. I did a lot of them, John. A lot of them. All over the country."

"It's okay."

"Okay? Yeah, it was okay. I could have kept going forever. Worked my way through every freak in the world. I never would have gotten sick. I was taking a lot of pills. For the pain. I had to keep moving, once I got started. I wasn't running from you anymore, just running. I had to do a lot of them before I'd find the right one. See his face. But once I got one done, I had to go. Right then, go." She took a deep breath. Something rattled inside her when she did it. "They knew about it. They had to know. They knew. One of them even asked me, are you her? They knew someone in the underground was killing them. But I never had any trouble getting clients. Never. I got bigger, stronger."

"I saw a picture," I told her.

"Yes?" she said. Then she closed her eyes. I thought she was going to sleep again. I sat there, watched her. Then she started talking again, but it was a whisper. Not like she was weak, just telling secrets.

"I got to need it. More and more. I saw his face all the time. Once I must have passed out when I did it. When I came to, he was there, all tied up and bloody. I left him there, went into the bathroom to take a shower. Then I saw it. Blood. On my mouth. All over my mouth. Then next time I did it, I stopped pretending. Stopped playing. I drank their blood. It was the best, sweetest, purest thing I ever did. That's how it must have happened."

It was getting dark in the room. When she went to sleep, I stayed right there.

♠

She didn't sleep so long. I had time, though. Time to think. When she opened her eyes, I told her.

"I can get you out of here," I said.

"What?"

"You can come with me. You don't have to . . . die here, Shella. We can go someplace. You can talk to me. Like it was. I can find him, too. Take him out before you go."

Her eyes were real soft, like they used to be, sometimes. I felt her hand on me. "Who, honey?"

"Your father. Like I promised."

"He's dead, baby. Long time dead. I found out. Once I started my march, I knew I could do him. Do him myself, the way it should be. He never left where he was—it was easy to find out. He just died. In his sleep. He was an old man. Just died. There's nothing left to do."

"We could still . . ."

"I don't want to be here. I don't want to go anyplace either. I want to be done. Out of this."

She looked at me. A hard straight look. Shella's look.

"One more deal, my partner. One more deal. You came a long way to hear. If I tell you what you want to know, will you do it?"

I lit a cigarette to get some time. She tapped my hand for a drag. I held it to her lips. She couldn't sit up anymore.

"Will you?"

I just nodded—I couldn't talk.

"I love you," Shella said.

Her neck snapped like a dry twig.

♠

I walked out the front door of the hospital. It was getting dark. The Jeep was sitting there. Like Duke's radio, with new batteries in it.

I got behind the wheel, started the engine. I sat there for a minute.

Then I put on the headlights and pulled out of the parking lot, driving slow.

When I got to the highway, I headed east.

Going to pick up my jacket.